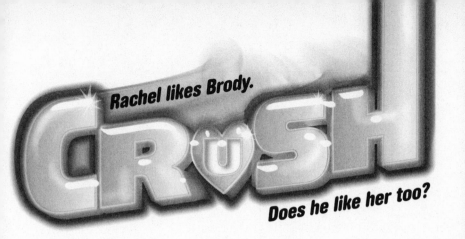

Rachel likes Brody.

Does he like her too?

Rachel's Valentine Crush
by Angela Darling

SIMON SPOTLIGHT
New York London Toronto Sydney New Delhi

This book is a work of fiction. Any references to historical events, real people, or real places are used fictitiously. Other names, characters, places, and events are products of the author's imagination, and any resemblance to actual events or places or persons, living or dead, is entirely coincidental.

SIMON SPOTLIGHT
An imprint of Simon & Schuster Children's Publishing Division
1230 Avenue of the Americas, New York, New York 10020
Copyright © 2013 by Simon & Schuster, Inc.
Text by Ellie O'Ryan
Designed by Dan Potash
All rights reserved, including the right of reproduction in whole or in part in any form.
SIMON SPOTLIGHT and colophon are registered trademarks of Simon & Schuster, Inc.
For information about special discounts for bulk purchases, please contact Simon & Schuster Special Sales at 1-866-506-1949 or business@simonandschuster.com.
Manufactured in the United States of America 1113 FFG
First Edition 10 9 8 7 6 5 4 3 2 1
ISBN 978-1-4424-8640-9 (pbk)
ISBN 978-1-4424-8641-6 (hc)
ISBN 978-1-4424-8642-3 (eBook)
Library of Congress Catalog Card Number 2012956185

chapter 1

"**COME ON, ROBBIE,**" **RACHEL PLEADED.** "**JUST EAT** two more bites of broccoli. That's it. Just two more bites."

"Peas, peas, peas," Rachel's little brother sang. "Peas, please. Peas, please."

"We don't have peas tonight," Rachel said for the hundredth time. "We have broccoli. Eat it up so you can have a special treat."

"Peas!" Robbie cried hopefully. He banged his fork on the table.

Rachel leaned toward the sink and turned the water on full blast so that Robbie wouldn't hear her groan.

Bzzzz!

"How's that broccoli coming?" Rachel called out as she dried her hands on her jeans. Then she pulled her cell out of her back pocket. She could already guess that the text was from her best friend, Taylor—even though

Rachel had specifically said that *she* would text Taylor as soon as she was ready. But Taylor wasn't exactly the patient type.

Rach! U ready?

"Peas!" Robbie hollered from the dining room.
"No, broccoli!" Rachel hollered back without looking up from her phone.

No! Still doing dishes and Robbie still eating. Going as fast as I can!!!

But it starts soooooon! Hurry hurry

Believe me, I know

Rachel's phone was already buzzing again as she shoved it back into her pocket, but she decided to ignore it—at least until Robbie finished eating. She suddenly realized that Robbie was quiet. Unusually quiet. Rachel peeked into the dining room, hoping to find his cheeks puffed out with a giant mouthful of broccoli. Instead, she found Robbie grinning at her with a broccoli floret sticking out of each ear.

"Robbie!" Rachel yelled. "You *know* you're not supposed to put food in your ears!"

Robbie's eyes widened.

Then, in a flash, he popped both broccoli bites into his mouth. Rachel blinked in surprise. She'd never seen Robbie eat his most hated food so fast.

"Tweat?" Robbie asked with his mouth full, spraying bits of broccoli onto the table.

"Okay, but chew with your mouth closed," Rachel replied as she ducked back into the kitchen. She stared into the pantry, knowing that her dad didn't like Robbie to eat a lot of sweets. It was the first time that Rachel had been responsible for Robbie's dinner and bedtime all by herself, and she really didn't want to mess it up.

Then again, sometimes Grandma Nellie gave Robbie a treat after dinner. Maybe she would've given him a little dessert tonight if she hadn't been at her Scrapbooking for Seniors meeting. So Rachel plucked three chocolate chips from a half-empty bag and brought them to Robbie.

"Here you go, buddy," she said. "Three chocolate chips for a three-year-old."

Robbie's whole face lit up as he shoved the chocolate chips into his mouth. "My chocolate yums!" he cried. "More, please!"

But Rachel had already whisked his plate off to the dishwasher. She glanced at the clock on the microwave; it read 7:46. She had fourteen minutes to finish the dishes and get Robbie to bed before *The Scoop* came on. Rachel had only watched the gossipy entertainment show once or twice; her dad thought TV shows like that were a giant waste of time. But Rachel hoped that he would make an exception tonight, since she had finished all her homework and her chores before the show started. After all, it wasn't every night that her former classmate, Brody Warner, was interviewed live on national TV!

Brody had been a singing superstar for almost nine months now, but Rachel was still amazed by everything that had happened. One day Brody was just a regular boy at her school, and the next he was a finalist on *SingNation!*, the most popular singing competition in the country. It didn't matter that Brody had come in second place; by the time the final episode aired, he had already become a household name. Of course, Rachel wasn't entirely surprised. She had been singing with Brody in their church choir since third grade, so Rachel had known for a long time just how talented Brody was.

A lot had changed since then. Rachel was now in seventh grade, and Brody would've been in eighth—if he hadn't moved to California to focus on his music career instead of going to Archer Middle School. It used to be that Rachel would sometimes see Brody around their town of Archer, Minnesota. These days, she still saw Brody's face all over town—on magazine covers, posters, and even T-shirts. But she hadn't seen Brody himself since he had flown out to Los Angeles to film *SingNation!* And, to be honest, Rachel missed him. She had just realized that she had a crush on Brody around the time when he auditioned for the show. And even though Brody had been gone for months, Rachel's feelings had only gotten stronger. That's why she was so excited to see Brody on TV tonight.

While Robbie licked the chocolate off his fingers, Rachel checked her cell. She had five new texts from Taylor.

Robbie done yet?

Hello?

Where did u go?

Did u drop ur phone in the disposal?

HELLOOOOOOOO????

Sorry, he just finished. Putting him 2 bed now

Want me 2 come over and help?

Yes but no. He loves u so much he would never go 2 sleep!!!

Lol let me know if i can help

Thx brb

"Okay, Robbie," Rachel said. "Time to brush your teeth!"

Rachel rushed through Robbie's bedtime routine as fast as she could. Then she sat very still in Robbie's dark bedroom as she waited for him to fall asleep. The minutes felt like hours. Rachel was dying to check her phone, but she worried that its glow would startle Robbie awake.

Then it would be impossible to get him back to sleep.

At last, it happened: Robbie's breathing became slow, deep, and even. Rachel crept out of his room as quietly as she could, stepping over the creaky board in the doorway. She pulled Robbie's door closed and did a silent fist pump in the hallway as she scurried back to the kitchen and started the dishwasher. It was 7:58.

ALL SET COME OVER!!

Taylor didn't even bother to text Rachel back. Thirty seconds later there was a soft knock at the front door. Rachel opened the door with a giant grin on her face. "Yayyyy!" she said. Then she reached out to brush some snowflakes from Taylor's bangs. "It's still snowing, huh?"

Taylor shrugged off her shiny fuchsia parka. "Yeah, and I forgot my hat. But I was in a hurry, you know?"

"Come on, I got the TV all set up," Rachel said as she led Taylor into the den. She paused to glance out the window at the falling snow. Her dad had been out plowing since early afternoon, but if it kept snowing like this, he might end up pulling a double shift.

"Oh, I almost forgot!" Taylor exclaimed as she held

up a paper bag. "Guess what I have!"

Rachel didn't need to look inside the bag to know what Taylor had brought. She could already smell the delicious scent of fresh-baked chocolate-chip cookies.

"My favorite," Rachel said. "You are so awesome!"

"Look! Look!" Taylor squealed, pointing at the muted TV. "It's starting!"

Both girls leaned forward excitedly as Rachel fumbled with the remote. Suddenly the sound of Brody's voice filled the living room. Rachel knew right away which song was playing—"Never Give Up." She'd listened to it on repeat about a thousand times since Brody's debut album had released last August.

"There he is!" Rachel whispered as she stared at the screen. Brody's closely cropped curly black hair was shining under the studio lights. The half smile on his face was a little shy, a little uncertain, and a lot adorable. There was no doubt about it: Brody was just as cute as the last time Rachel had seen him in person.

Maybe even cuter!

"Hi, girls."

Rachel spun around to see her dad standing in the doorway.

"Dad! Hi!" Rachel exclaimed as she scrambled up. The remote control clattered to the floor. Taylor lunged for it and paused the show so that Rachel wouldn't miss anything.

"Hi, Mr. Wilson," Taylor spoke up. "Want a cookie? I baked them after dinner. They're still warm."

"That sounds great," Mr. Wilson said as he crossed the room and reached for one of the cookies. "What are you watching?"

"Oh. It's just this show. It's called, um, *The Scoop*," Rachel said in a rush. "You remember Brody Warner? From church? And he used to go to our school? He's, like, this big superstar singer now, so he's on the show tonight and we thought we'd watch it. Just because we know him. Is that okay?"

"What time does it end?" Mr. Wilson asked as he glanced at his watch.

"The show ends at eight-thirty, and I finished all my homework," Rachel replied. "Also, Robbie is asleep. He ate every bite of his dinner—even the broccoli. And I did the dishes. So I was, um, kind of hoping I could watch the show. Just this once."

"Great job, Rachel, thank you," Mr. Wilson told

her. Then he turned to Taylor. "And it's okay with your parents?"

Taylor nodded vigorously. "Yeah, they said it was fine as long as I come home right after it ends."

"All right then, you can watch it," Mr. Wilson replied, stifling a yawn. "Rach, I'm going to bed. It looks like this snow is going to pick up, so I volunteered for another shift tonight."

"Do you think we'll have a snow day tomorrow?" Taylor asked hopefully.

A smile crossed Mr. Wilson's tired face. "Not if I can help it," he joked. "Enjoy your show, girls."

"Good night, Dad," Rachel said. She watched her father rub his sore neck as he left the den. For the past eight years Mr. Wilson had run his own landscaping business. During the warmer months he spent long hours working outside: designing gardens, planting trees, and maintaining lawns. But in the winter, when it was too cold for gardening, he drove a snowplow for the city. Sometimes he was out all night in the bitter cold to make sure that the streets were clear in the morning.

As Rachel sat down again, Taylor pressed play, and *The Scoop* began at last.

"He's young. He's popular. And his debut album, *Out of Bounds*, has sold more than two million copies in six months, with three number-one singles," the announcer, Melanie Martinez, said as photos of Brody flashed across the screen. "And with all that to his credit, he's just fourteen years old. Who is he? None other than Brody Warner, the hottest pop star in the nation! And tonight, you'll find him right here in our studio, answering all your questions on *The Scoop* . . . live!"

Rachel couldn't help herself. She squealed a little as she bounced up and down.

"Shhh! Shhh!" Taylor said through her giggles. "Don't wake up Robbie. Or your dad!"

"You're right," Rachel replied as she reached for a cookie. If her mouth was full, hopefully she wouldn't start freaking out in the middle of Brody's interview.

"But first," Melanie continued, "we have *The Scoop* on the shocking season finale of *Famous Friends*. Jackson Barnes has the latest. Jackson?"

Rachel groaned. "Who *cares* about *Famous Friends*?" she asked. "I want just want to hear about *our* famous friend. When are they going to get to the good stuff?"

"Probably not until the end," Taylor said. "They know

that's all anybody cares about, so they're gonna make us wait. But lucky for us, we're delayed a little from our chat with your dad."

Taylor fast-forwarded for a few moments until Brody appeared on the screen again. He was sitting on a sleek leather couch across from Melanie Martinez. Rachel, her eyes glued to the screen, started chewing on her cuticles.

"Brody, thanks for joining us tonight," Melanie said warmly. "I know this must be a crazy time for you—your second album, *Songs from My Heart*, drops at midnight, and we're really happy that you could be here with us when you've got so much going on."

"Oh, sure. I mean, no problem," Brody said. He looked down shyly for half a second—long enough to make Rachel's heart skip a beat. "Anything for my fans, you know?"

Melanie's superwhite teeth gleamed as she laughed a little too hard. "So tell us, Brody, about your new album," she continued. "*Songs from My Heart*. Sounds intense . . . and romantic. Is it?"

"Well, yeah," Brody replied. "It means a lot to me because I wrote or cowrote all the songs on it. And that was a really amazing experience, you know—to have this music in my head, and actually write it down, and then find the right words to go with it. Everything about the songs is true. They really do come from my heart."

"It sounds like a very personal project," Melanie said. "A real labor of love."

"Yes, definitely."

"So let's talk about love," Melanie said, switching gears.

Rachel sat up a little straighter on the couch. She had *not* expected this.

"When I first heard the title of your new album, I had to wonder if there was a special someone you had in mind when you came up with it," Melanie continued. "And I know I'm not alone. When we invited your fans to send us their burning questions for you, they overwhelmingly asked if you're single!"

Brody laughed nervously. His coffee-brown eyes darted to the side for just a moment, as if he were trying to ask someone offscreen for help.

"I'm thinking, specifically, of 'Secret Crush,'" Melanie pressed on. "Wow, what a song, Brody. You really knocked it out of the park. So from what you said earlier, am I right to assume that it was written about a particular girl?"

Brody opened his mouth to answer and then closed it again. He coughed lightly and politely covered his mouth with his hand, then proceeded to fidget with the collar of his shirt.

He's totally nervous! Rachel thought. She had never seen Brody look so uncomfortable . . . yet so totally adorable at the same time.

The pause before Brody spoke seemed like an eternity. Finally, he smiled sheepishly at Melanie. "You guessed right," he said. "I do have a secret crush."

Melanie clapped her hands together. "Yes! I knew it!" she cried. "Tell us more, Brody. Who is she?"

But Brody pressed his lips together and shook his head. "I can't," he said. "If I did, it wouldn't be a secret."

"Now, Brody, you can't do that to us!" Melanie said playfully. "Your fans want to know!"

Brody looked offscreen again. "I guess I can tell you this . . . ," he said slowly. "There's a special message to her in 'Secret Crush.' So hopefully—if she listens to the song, I mean—she'll know that it's about her."

"How mysterious," Melanie said. "But surely you can give us a few more clues, Brody. Did you meet her on tour? Is she from your hometown? What are her initials?"

"I, uh—" Brody began.

"At least tell us *which* line of the song has the secret message!" Melanie interrupted him.

Brody was speechless. Once more he cast a desperate glance offscreen. Then, to Rachel's surprise, a man entered the shot and sat next to Brody.

"Melanie, sorry for the interruption," the man said smoothly. "I'm Greg Pierce, Brody's manager. And while Brody's not going to make any announcements about his secret crush tonight, he does have some big news he can share."

Greg turned to Brody and gave him an encouraging grin. "Go ahead, Brody—tell them about the decision that we made just this morning."

Brody relaxed a little and smiled into the camera. "Well, the *Songs from My Heart* tour was supposed to begin in Houston in March," he said. "But when we thought about it, we decided that the best time to kick off the tour would be on Valentine's Day. So I'm psyched to announce that we've added a new concert to the schedule—and it's going to be in my hometown!"

Rachel clapped her hands over her mouth. She wanted to scream with excitement! Brody's last tour had taken him around the whole country, but he'd never performed a concert in Archer before.

"And that's not all," Greg continued, "because at the special Valentine's Day concert, Brody will finally tell the world the true identity of his secret crush!"

There was a moment of stunned silence on the set— and in Rachel's den, too.

"Whoa-whoa-whoa-whoa-whoa," Taylor said in a low voice. "Did I hear that right? *Brody* is coming *here* on *Valentine's Day* to tell everyone who he *likes*?"

But Rachel didn't respond. She couldn't take her eyes off Brody's face—he looked shocked, and even a little scared. *Was that really part of their plan?* she wondered. Because Brody looked as surprised as she felt.

Before Brody could speak, Melanie turned to face the camera. "Breaking news, brought to you only on *The Scoop,*" she said breathlessly. "Brody Warner will reveal his secret crush at a special Valentine's Day concert!"

A sheepish smile spread across Brody's face. "I'm really excited about playing in my hometown," he said, obviously trying to direct the subject away from his crush. "We have a great show planned."

"Tickets go on sale in two hours," added his manager.

"Exciting times for Brody Warner," Melanie said. "A new album, a big tour, a surprise announcement, and a secret crush—soon to be revealed to the world! Thanks so much for being here tonight, Brody, and for our fans at home, remember to always turn to *The Scoop* for the latest news about all your favorite stars, including the one and only Brody Warner!"

Rachel still didn't say anything as she reached for the remote. Her mind was spinning as one thought repeated again and again: *Could I be Brody's secret crush? Could I be Brody's secret crush?*

No. No way. It was impossible. Sure, Brody had always been nice to her—but that was just his personality. Brody was nice to *everybody*.

But as much as Rachel tried to tell herself that Brody was obviously talking—and singing—about some other girl, a little voice in the back of her head was asking *What if? Maybe I* am *his secret crush!* she thought giddily. *Maybe it's me!*

Rachel's eyes were shining as she turned to Taylor.

"Can you even believe it?" Taylor asked in an excited whisper so that she wouldn't wake up Rachel's dad and brother. "Can you *even* believe it?"

CRUSH

"I'm sorry, am I dreaming?" Rachel asked. "Did that really just happen?"

"It did!" Taylor exclaimed. "It so did! Rach, do you know what this *means*? Brody's crushing on a girl from our school! It might be—it might be you!"

"No, it's not me," Rachel said automatically. "And just because the concert is going to be here doesn't mean she lives here. They could bring her in for the concert."

Taylor shook her head emphatically. "Then why would they move the concert to Archer? They could just keep it in Houston."

"That's a good point," Rachel replied.

"Ugh, *why* did I spend all my birthday money already?" asked Taylor. "I really want to go to the concert, but I just know the tickets are going to be insanely expensive."

"Probably," Rachel said. But for her, it wouldn't matter how much the tickets cost. She couldn't imagine that her dad would ever give her permission to attend an actual pop concert. He hadn't even let Rachel go to the pool party Brody had thrown during his one visit to Archer last August. "Maybe the concert will be on TV or something. We could have a sleepover!"

"That would be cool," Taylor replied. "Definitely better

18

than last year's Valentine's Day. That was the *worst*, just sitting in class all day wishing that somebody would send me a candy-gram. I can't believe it's a whole year later and I'm still totally invisible to every single boy at school."

"You don't know that," Rachel argued. "Maybe somebody likes you and he's too shy to say it. Besides, there isn't anybody you like right now . . . is there?"

"Not really," Taylor admitted. "But it would still be nice to know that somebody likes *me*. You're so lucky, Rachel—I mean, what if you really *are* Brody's crush?"

"That's doubtful," Rachel replied. "But I still can't wait to hear 'Secret Crush.' I'm totally staying up till midnight to download it!"

"Me too," Taylor agreed as she reached for her coat. "I want to hear the secret message that Brody has for you!"

"Whatever," Rachel said, but she couldn't stop smiling. "I wish you didn't have to go. I wish we were having a sleepover tonight so that we could listen to the album together."

"I know!" Taylor said. "Stupid Monday night release. Who thought *that* was a good idea?"

Rachel and Taylor were extra quiet as they walked down the hallway. At the front door Rachel whispered,

"Thanks for coming over. And thanks for the cookies!"

"If you figure out the secret message, text me *immediately*," Taylor whispered back. "I don't even care if it's three o'clock in the morning. I want to know."

"You got it," Rachel giggled as Taylor walked outside. Rachel watched through the window while Taylor trudged home in the swirling snow. Once again she was grateful that her best friend lived next door—and even more grateful that her best friend was someone like Taylor.

The freezing air seeped in through the windowpane, making Rachel shiver. As soon as Taylor walked into her own house, Rachel went to the kitchen to make a cup of hot chocolate. In just a few hours, she would be listening to Brody's new album and maybe—*maybe*—finding out if he liked her, too.

And Rachel could hardly wait!

chapter 2

JUST BEFORE TEN O'CLOCK RACHEL HEARD THE
sound of Grandma Nellie's car pulling into the driveway.
A few moments later there was a soft tap at Rachel's
door.

"Come in," she said quietly.

"Hi, peach pie," Grandma Nellie said from the doorway,
using the nickname she'd had for Rachel since she was a
baby. "I saw your light on. What are you doing up?"

Rachel glanced down shyly. "Brody's new album
comes out at midnight, so I wanted to stay up to download
it," she explained.

Grandma Nellie smiled knowingly. Rachel had never
explained her feelings for Brody, but somehow Grandma
Nellie seemed to know all about them. But Grandma Nellie
always followed Rachel's lead—she never made a big deal
about it or teased Rachel about her crush.

"How was your scrapbooking club?" Rachel asked, changing the subject.

Grandma Nellie's eyes lit up. "Oh, we had the best time," she said. "And I finished two new pages! I'd show them to you right now but the glue is still wet. I barely got them home without wrecking them."

"Can I see them in the morning?" Rachel asked.

"Absolutely," Grandma Nellie said, nodding. She sat at the foot of Rachel's bed. "How did Robbie do tonight?"

"He was great," Rachel said, stifling a yawn. "No trouble. He even ate the broccoli."

"Impressive!" Grandma Nellie said. "Of course, he'd do anything for the world's best big sister."

Rachel's father appeared in the doorway, looking sleepy. "What's this? A slumber party?" he asked.

"Oh, I'm sorry, Carl," Grandma Nellie said. "Did we wake you?"

"I heard voices . . . ," Mr. Wilson began. Then he turned to Rachel. "It's past your bedtime, young lady. Why are you awake?"

"I was—there's this thing I need to do—to download," Rachel began. "An album. But it isn't available until midnight, so I thought I'd stay up."

Mr. Wilson shook his head. "Midnight? On a school night? No way," he replied. "Time to shut down that computer, kiddo. Lights out in five minutes."

He didn't sound mad, but his voice was firm. Rachel knew that she didn't have a choice. "Okay, Dad," she said. "Sorry if we woke you up."

"That's okay." Mr. Wilson crossed the room and gave Rachel a kiss on the forehead. "Good night, sweetie. Come on, Mom, let's let Rachel get some sleep. It's a school night, after all."

"Night, Dad. Night, Grandma Nellie," Rachel said as she watched them leave. In the doorway, Grandma Nellie paused for a moment to mouth *Sorry!* to Rachel. Rachel smiled and blew her a kiss. It wasn't Grandma Nellie's fault that Dad had woken up . . . or that he was so strict.

After she shut down her computer, Rachel made sure to set her alarm for five a.m. She wasn't going to disobey her father and stay up late to download Brody's song . . . but he hadn't said anything about waking up early!

Usually the first thing Rachel did on a winter morning was check to see if she had a snow day. But when her alarm started beeping, Rachel leaped out of bed and rushed over to her laptop. Using a gift card that she had been saving since Christmas, Rachel immediately downloaded *Songs from My Heart*. She drummed her fingers on her desk impatiently. Even though it was still dark outside, Rachel was already wide awake—in fact, she was so jittery it was hard to sit still. In just moments, she would be listening "Secret Crush"!

While she waited for the album to finish downloading, Rachel got up and started pacing around her room. She peeked out the window and saw that the snow had finally stopped falling. Since her dad's truck was gone, Rachel figured that he and all of the other plow drivers were still working to clear the back roads. But the street in front of her house was clear. From the look of it, school would definitely be in session today. When Rachel's computer started beeping, though, she forgot all about school: The download was complete!

Rachel rushed over to her laptop and put on her headphones so that the music wouldn't wake Robbie or Grandma Nellie. A grin spread over her face as she looked at the screen. There were twelve brand-new Brody Warner songs waiting for her! And Rachel knew exactly which one she would listen to first. As the opening notes of "Secret Crush" swelled through her headphones, Rachel closed her eyes and listened carefully.

I have a secret
It's hidden in my heart
And it's only getting bigger
Since we have been apart
Maybe it's crazy
To feel the way I do
But you're my secret crush
And I wish you liked me, too

Walkin' in the springtime
You shine just like the sun
And when I think about you
Girl, I know that you're the one
Maybe it's crazy
To feel the way I do
But you're my secret crush
And I dream you like me, too

I think about the best times
Making music together

And how much I miss you
Want to hold your hand forever
Maybe it's crazy
To feel the way I do
But you're my secret crush
And I hope you like me, too

Oh, Brody! Rachel thought giddily. She wrapped her arms around her legs and rested her chin on her knees, beaming with happiness. Rachel was so impressed by "Secret Crush"—and even more impressed that Brody had written it himself. He was obviously so talented. There was no question that "Secret Crush" was a great song. It was different from most of the songs on Brody's first album—a little slower, a little softer. Rachel listened to it again and could tell, without a doubt, that the song really had come from Brody's heart.

On her second listen, Rachel noticed something new. At the very end of "Secret Crush," Brody said . . . something. Rachel frowned with concentration as she listened to the ending for a third time. But the recording wasn't very clear. All Rachel knew for sure was that Brody was speaking. *Could that be the secret message?* she wondered. *No, it has to be in the lyrics. Brody was talking about how much writing the lyrics meant to him. That's got to be where he put the clue about his crush.*

And that made hope stir in Rachel's heart as she listened to the song again and again. Most of the lyrics were pretty vague; Rachel hated to admit it, but they could be about anyone. Brody didn't even get specific about his crush's hair or eye color. But there was one part of the song that caught Rachel's attention:

> *I think about the best times*
> *Making music together*

Those lines made Rachel think of singing in the church choir with Brody. Sure, the songs they sang in choir were nothing like the pop songs that had turned Brody into a superstar. But the melodies were achingly lovely, and sometimes when the choir practiced in the sanctuary, all their voices seemed to spiral up toward the steeple, mingling with the colored light that streamed through the stained-glass windows. In those moments Rachel felt like singing was the most perfect, most meaningful, most beautiful thing she could do.

Maybe Brody had felt that way too.

And if he did—*if he did!*—then maybe Rachel really was Brody's secret crush!

The thought made Rachel so giddy that she could hardly stop smiling as she listened to "Secret Crush" on repeat. The more she listened to it, the more Rachel was convinced: The secret message was for her. It made perfect sense!

Rachel jumped when she felt a tap on her shoulder. She turned around to see Grandma Nellie standing behind her.

"Morning!" Rachel exclaimed as she pulled her headphones off.

"Sorry to barge in—I knocked on the door, but I guess you didn't hear me with the headphones," Grandma Nellie said. Her eyes twinkled. "How's the new music?"

"Perfect," Rachel sighed happily. "It's really, really good."

"What a talented young man," Grandma Nellie said. "Later, you'll have to play your favorite song for me. But right now it's breakfast time, peach pie. You don't want to be late for school."

"Whoops," Rachel replied. "I almost forgot!"

"See you in the kitchen," Grandma Nellie said as she

left, closing Rachel's door behind her.

Rachel dressed in her most comfortable jeans and an indigo sweater that had been her favorite Christmas present. She was so happy today that she wanted to look extra nice at school. After pulling her hair back with a skinny silver headband, Rachel hurried off to breakfast. There was a big pot of oatmeal steaming on the kitchen table, next to a pitcher of maple syrup and a jar of cinnamon. Robbie was already hard at work on his oatmeal. He even had some in his hair! Rachel grabbed a wet paper towel to get it out before it dried.

"It stopped snowing, but it is *freezing* outside," Grandma Nellie said as she ladled some oatmeal into a bowl for Rachel. "So eat a nice big breakfast today, Rachel."

"You got it, Grandma Nellie," Rachel replied. "Hey! Weren't you going to show me your scrapbook pages?"

"I thought you'd never ask," Grandma Nellie teased as she wiped her hands on a dishtowel. Then she carefully brought two bright-aqua sheets of cardstock over to the table. "What do you think?"

"Grandma Nellie! They're *awesome*!" Rachel exclaimed. And she really meant it too. The scrapbook pages chronicled a cross-country road trip that

Grandma Nellie had taken right after high school. Grandma Nellie had pasted several grainy-looking photos of her trip onto the pages and written short descriptions about each one. She'd also added post cards, souvenirs, and an old map that she had saved for more than fifty years. "I can't believe how long your hair was back then."

"Neither can I," Grandma Nellie said, laughing. She reached up and ran her fingers through her short gray curls. "It used to take me hours to style it like that. These days, I figure I have more important things to do."

"Like scrapbooking?" asked Rachel.

Grandma Nellie nodded. "For my whole life, I've been saving my mementos in shoeboxes," she told Rachel. "I never quite knew what to do with them. But gosh, honey, it sure is fun to unpack those boxes and have all these memories come rushing back. And speaking of rushing . . ."

Rachel glanced at the clock on the microwave. "7:10!" she gasped as the doorbell rang. "Aaaah, that's Taylor! I've gotta go or we'll *both* be late!"

chapter 3

RACHEL GAVE ROBBIE AND GRANDMA NELLIE A
pair of quick kisses and threw on her lilac parka. Then
she grabbed her backpack and dashed out the front door,
where Taylor was waiting impatiently.

"*You* were supposed to text me when you figured
out the secret message!" Taylor said accusingly. "At
midnight!"

Rachel's hands flew up to her face. "I *totally* forgot!"
she exclaimed. "I'm so sorry, T. If it makes you feel any
better, my dad didn't even let me stay up until midnight.
So I was actually asleep."

Taylor looked grumpy for two more seconds before
she burst out laughing. "My parents didn't let me stay up
late, either," she admitted. "So I didn't even get to listen
to the album until this morning. How awesome is it?!"

"The awesomest," Rachel replied. That same

involuntary smile flitted across her face before she could help herself. Taylor figured out what it meant right away.

"You know something!" she shrieked. "Tell me! What's the clue in 'Secret Crush'?"

"Well, I don't know for sure," Rachel said. "I just—it's a great song, isn't it?"

"Yes, it's the greatest, it's a masterpiece, Brody's a musical genius," Taylor said impatiently. "But why are you smiling like that?"

They were getting close to school, so Rachel glanced around to make sure no one could overhear her. "You have to promise you won't tell anyone," she began.

"Well, *duh*," Taylor replied at once.

"No, I mean really, really promise, like swear-on-your-life-and-hope-to-die promise," said Rachel.

"Rachel. Of course I won't tell anyone," Taylor said.

And Rachel knew that she wouldn't. "So, you know that line about making music together?" she asked.

Taylor thought for a moment. "Um, yeah. I remember."

"I think that's the clue!" Rachel exclaimed. "And . . . Taylor . . . I think it might be . . . about *me*—since Brody and I were in choir together!"

Taylor squealed so loudly that Rachel grabbed her

arm and shushed her. Then Rachel started giggling. She couldn't help it—she was just too happy to worry about drawing attention to herself.

"But I don't want everybody to know," Rachel continued. "Just in case I'm wrong. That would be so embarrassing."

"No worries. I won't say a word," Taylor promised.

But the minute the girls walked into school, it was clear that everyone else was already talking about "Secret Crush." Excited chatter buzzed through the halls. Groups of students stood together to listen to Brody's new album on someone's phone. Rachel immediately noticed that a large crowd had gathered around Tammy Hemmings's locker. Tammy was the most beautiful, popular girl in eighth grade—maybe in the whole school. Normally Rachel didn't try to listen in on other people's conversations, but the way everyone was clustered around Tammy made her curious. If Brody had stayed at Archer Middle School, he would've been in eighth grade this year too. Maybe the older kids knew something about him that Rachel didn't.

"I think the clue is in the sunshine line," Amber Jones said. "Come on, that's definitely about the seventh-grade class picnic last spring, don't you think?"

Becca Morrison shook her head. "No way. It was only sunny for part of the picnic. The rest of the time we thought it was going to start raining."

"None of those lines really seemed like clues to me," Clarissa Chow pointed out. "Except for that one about 'making music.' Am I right, Tammy?"

Tammy checked her reflection in her locker mirror. She carefully applied some shiny pink lip gloss before she answered. "Well, I *think* so," she said slowly. "Because Brody and I spent a ton of time together in glee club. Especially when we were practicing for our all-state solos."

Rachel felt a sharp twinge in the center of her chest. *Glee club. All-state solos,* she thought numbly. *How could I forget?*

Ever since she had started middle school, Rachel had wanted to be in glee club too. But her father wouldn't allow it. He wanted Rachel to come right home after school so that she could focus on her homework and help take care of Robbie. And even though Rachel would've loved to be in glee club—especially after she started crushing on Brody—she was grateful that her dad let her be in the church choir. That chance to sing was the best part of her week.

And why wouldn't Brody have a crush on Tammy? Rachel asked herself. *She's so popular and pretty. Practically every boy in school likes her!*

"It's not something that everybody knows about," Tammy continued, smiling. "But Brody and I spent *so* much time together practicing those solos. We had this really strong, like, connection. I'm pretty sure I was the first person that he told about getting to compete on *SingNation!* And, I mean, I don't want to brag, but I *always* knew that he was going to go really far. He's crazy talented, you know? I remember at the end of our practice sessions, we would hang out together while we waited for the late bus, and sometimes we would sing a little duet . . . it was really magical."

"Sooo romantic," Marisol Hernandez said with a sigh. "Were you guys secretly dating?"

Tammy shook her head. "See, that's the thing," she said, lowering her voice a little. "We had this connection, but Brody never asked me out or anything. I know he's on TV now and he plays these giant sold-out shows, but one-on-one, he can be kind of shy. So, honestly, it wouldn't surprise me at all if he had a secret crush on me."

Rachel turned away. She had heard enough. But then she heard something that made her pause.

"I just don't think that line about 'making music' is the clue, though," said Gabriella Bruno. "It's gotta be that part at the end—when Brody stops singing and talks instead."

"I couldn't understand him," Marisol replied. "What *did* he say?"

"That's why it's the clue!" Gabriella said excitedly. "It's not supposed to be *easy* to figure out."

"Wasn't it, like, L-O-L?" asked Clarissa. "You have to turn it up at the end to really hear it, but he says something about L-O-L."

"I think the line is, 'I will always something-something L-O-L something-something you,'" Gabriella said. "I listened to it over and over this morning."

"L-O-L? Laughing out loud is not that romantic," Becca said, a skeptical look on her face.

"No way. My big sister *only* goes out with guys who are funny," Amber disagreed. "She says that a sense of humor is just as important as being cute. Besides, Brody and I were laughing together a *ton* at the seventh-grade picnic."

"So you think the song is about *you*?" Tammy asked,

acting surprised. She didn't say it in a mean way, exactly, but it was enough to make Amber look at the ground in embarrassment.

"Does L-O-L mean anything to you?" Marisol asked Tammy. "Did you and Brody laugh together a lot at glee club?"

Tammy smiled again. "Absolutely. We goofed around all the time. I listened to that line a couple times too. I think he says, 'I'll always share L-O-L times with you.' It's just Brody's way of saying that he'll always make time to laugh with me—no matter how famous or busy he gets."

As the other girls started to talk all at once, Rachel finally walked away. She approached her locker on autopilot, hardly aware of all the commotion in the hall around her.

"Rach! Rach! Wait up!" Taylor called behind her. "What's wrong? You just disappeared."

Rachel focused very hard on dialing her combination. "Sorry, T," she said quietly. "I didn't mean to ditch you. I just . . . I couldn't listen to that anymore."

"What do you mean?" Taylor asked. Then her eyes grew wide. "Oh, seriously? You think *Brody* likes *Tammy*?"

Rachel just shrugged.

"Oh, *whatever*," Taylor said. "Come on, Rach. Don't get sucked into that. Tammy didn't say one single thing that convinced me."

"You're just trying to make me feel better," said Rachel.

"No, I'm just telling you the truth," Taylor replied firmly.

"But what about glee club? That's probably what the 'making music' line is about," Rachel said glumly.

"It could just as easily be about church choir," countered Taylor.

"Well, what about the L-O-L thing?" Rachel said.

"Did you and Brody joke around at choir?" asked Taylor.

"No way. Goofing around is *definitely* not allowed. Besides, we practice in a church. It's not really the best place for cracking jokes," Rachel said miserably. "I have to go back and listen to that line with the volume up, but I think they're right that he says something about L-O-L. And if that's the case, he definitely wasn't talking about me."

For a moment Taylor looked stumped. Then she

shook her head. "I'm still not convinced that Tammy's right. I mean, 'I'll always share L-O-L times with you?' Who talks like that? That doesn't even make any sense!"

A faint smile flickered across Rachel's face. "Thanks for trying to make me feel better," she said. "But if Brody likes Tammy, I'd rather face it now. There's no point in getting my hopes up for nothing. That will only make it worse when . . ."

Rachel's voice trailed off. She didn't even want to say it. But she could tell that Taylor knew what she was thinking: *when Brody tells everybody that Tammy is his secret crush.*

Rachel tried to act normally for the rest of the school day, but it wasn't easy. More than anything, she wanted to hole up in her room, alone, where she could feel as sad as she wanted without worrying about what everyone else would think. While she was stuck in school, Rachel wanted to forget about "Secret Crush"—and Brody Warner—as much as she could. But it soon became clear that would be impossible. Almost every girl in seventh and eighth grade suddenly had a story about the time she and Brody had laughed together about something. By lunchtime most kids agreed that the LOL line was the clue.

But Rachel still wasn't entirely convinced. When she listened to that line again, it didn't really sound like "share L-O-L times." Even so, Rachel kept peeking over at Tammy during lunch—the way she tossed back her long copper-colored hair, the way she smiled at everyone like they were her new best friend. It was hard to think of a reason why Brody *wouldn't* have a crush on her.

Finally the school day ended, and Taylor and Rachel walked home together. Rachel was grateful that Taylor carried on most of the conversation herself. Rachel had been faking a good mood for so long that she was practically out of energy. When she got home, Robbie was waiting for her inside the front door.

"Rachel's home! Rachel's home! Rachel! Rachel!" he cried happily. He drove a dump truck into her foot. "Play trucks with me!"

Rachel reached down to tousle his hair and move the truck out of her way. "Maybe in a little while, Robbie," she said. "I have to get started on my homework."

"Is it truck homework?" Robbie asked hopefully.

"No, it's algebra," Rachel replied, smiling in spite of her lousy day. "A special kind of math. You know, numbers. But I can definitely play trucks with you before dinner."

Satisfied, Robbie drove his truck down the hall, and Rachel went straight to her room. Usually she would go to the kitchen for a snack and a chat with Grandma Nellie, but right now Rachel wanted to be alone—for a few minutes, at least.

But Rachel had hardly flopped down on her bed before there was a knock at the door. "Come in," she called in a weary voice.

Grandma Nellie poked her head into the room. "No snack?" she started to say. Then she caught a glimpse of Rachel's face. "What's wrong, sweet pea?"

Rachel shrugged. "I've just had a long day," she replied. It was technically the truth—she had been awake since five a.m.

"I see," Grandma Nellie said. She was quiet for a long moment, and Rachel got the feeling that Grandma Nellie was trying to figure out a way to make her feel better, even though she didn't know exactly what was wrong. Finally she snapped her fingers like an idea had just occurred to her. "Well, come here for just a minute. There's something I want to show you."

Rachel followed Grandma Nellie down the hall to the oak cabinet that stood outside her bedroom. Grandma Nellie flung open the doors to reveal stacks of neatly organized art supplies. "I spent all morning sorting through my scrapbooking stuff," Grandma Nellie said proudly.

Rachel gazed at the pile of smooth multicolored cardstock, a box of rubber stamps and ink pads, jars of sparkly glitter arranged in a pyramid, and sheets of shiny foil that reflected her face in rainbow colors. "Looks good, Grandma Nellie," she said. "Now you can do even more scrapbooking."

"And so can you!" Grandma Nellie replied as she pulled out a blank scrapbook for Rachel. "You should give it a try, peach pie. You're so creative and talented, and it's a really fun way to express yourself."

Rachel glanced into the cupboard again. Part of her was definitely drawn to the colorful supplies—but part of her resisted. If her dad saw her working on an art project with stamps and glitter glue, he would definitely not think she was mature. "Doesn't it seem . . . kind of like kid stuff?" Rachel asked, without thinking about how that sounded.

Grandma Nellie raised her eyebrows in surprise. "Kid stuff? Do I look like a kid to you?" she asked.

Rachel smiled sheepishly. "Sorry, Grandma Nellie."

"I'm just teasing you, sweetheart," Grandma Nellie replied. "I only wish I had started when I was your age. I think scrapbooking is a really great way of capturing your memories . . . and even figuring out your feelings. You see these lined pages?" She scanned the cupboard and pulled out some pretty pink pages with lines on them, sort of like fancy notebook paper. "You can use these special sheets of paper to write down stories or memories and then paste them down in the scrapbook. That's not something a little kid could do, now, is it?"

Grandma Nellie pulled a few more items from the cupboard and piled them on top of the blank scrapbook: a purple gel pen, a jar of purple glitter, and a small bottle of clear glue. "Why don't you take these back to your room?" she said. "Just in case inspiration strikes. If you don't end up using them, you can always just put them back. No pressure . . . but I think you'll find that you really like it if you give it a try."

"Okay." Rachel gave in. "Thanks, Grandma Nellie."

"If you get hungry, I made peanut-butter bars,"

Grandma Nellie told her. "But I can't guarantee that they'll last until dinner. Robbie is a fiend for peanut butter."

"Don't I know it," Rachel agreed.

She carried the supplies back to her room and put them on her desk. Next, Rachel cued up "Secret Crush." It was just as good as she remembered.

Rachel twirled the gel pen in her fingers for a moment, deep in thought. Then she rummaged around in the secret inside pocket of her backpack. Her fingers closed around a crinkly piece of cellophane. After spending months in her backpack, the printing on the label was completely worn off. Rachel knew it was silly to keep an old lollipop wrapper—let alone carry it around in her backpack. But it was special to her, and she never wanted to get rid of it.

Rachel smoothed the wrapper out on her desk. She chose a fresh sheet of pink lined paper from the top of the pile and paused for only a moment before she started writing. She had a really important memory she wanted to get down on paper.

It started out like a regular choir practice—we warmed up while Mr. Jenkins played some scales, and then we started singing hymns. It

44

was early April, just a few weeks before Brody left for SingNation!

When practice ended, Mr. Jenkins had this giant smile on his face when he brought out the lollipops. The lollipops are a thing that Mr. Jenkins does after every practice. They're made for singers and actors and people who use their voices a lot. They really do soothe my throat after I've been singing for a couple hours, and the green ones taste ah-maaaaazing. Way better than the red ones or the orange ones (gross!). I always try to grab a green one, but Mr. Jenkins says, "No digging around for your favorite color," so I have to be fast. And this time I accidentally picked a red one. It wasn't the end of the world—I mean, at least it wasn't orange! But I still wished that I had gotten a green one.

Then the craziest thing happened. I couldn't believe it then, and I still kind of can't believe it now (that's why I saved the wrapper all this time). Brody came up and tapped me on the shoulder. When I turned around and saw him, I couldn't even say anything, I was so surprised. And he was smiling—he has the cutest smile I have ever seen!!—as he held out a green lollipop.

"Trade?" he asked.

I just stood there with this dumb smile on my face until I was finally able to say, "Sure. You don't mind?"

Brody shook his head. I think I was blushing. I know I was trying superhard not to say or do something stupid or stare at him or anything embarrassing like that.

"I noticed that you always pick the green ones," he said.

"Thanks, Brody," I said. I think that was all I said. And we both just kind of grinned at each other for a moment before he said, "See ya," and left. For the rest of the day, I kept remembering what he said: I noticed that you always pick the green ones.

He noticed.

He noticed me!!!

Rachel sat back and read what she had written. Grandma Nellie was right: Somehow, writing down her memory made her feel a lot better about everything. She carefully glued the lined page to the center of the scrapbook page. Then she glued the lollipop wrapper to the bottom corner of the page and used the glitter to add sparkly swirls and hearts around it.

Rachel sat back and surveyed her work. It looked pretty good, if she did say so herself!

Maybe Brody does like Tammy, Rachel thought as she capped the glitter. *But . . . maybe . . . there's still a chance he likes me.*

chapter 4

THE NEXT MORNING RACHEL FIGURED THAT THE
other kids at school wouldn't be talking about Brody
quite so much. There wasn't a lot more to analyze about
the lyrics to "Secret Crush," and from the texts she had
received the night before, Rachel could tell that her
classmates were getting a little bored with trying to figure
out the hidden clue in the song.

Then came homeroom.

"For our seventh- and eighth-grade classes, I have
some big news!" the principal, Ms. Gutierrez, announced
over the loudspeaker. "Last night, Brody Warner's
representatives contacted me and very generously invited
all the seventh and eighth graders to Brody's special
Valentine's Day show at the Archer Arena!"

Ms. Gutierrez said something else, though Rachel
couldn't hear her over the screams of excitement

echoing up and down the corridor. When the noise finally died down, Ms. Gutierrez continued with the rest of the announcements—but Rachel still couldn't hear a word. This time, though, she was distracted by her own thoughts.

Tickets for everyone! Rachel thought gleefully. *I can't believe it! I've never been to a real concert before. This is going to be so, so, so amazing. . . . I have no idea what to wear. . . . Oh wow, I'll finally get to go to one of Brody's concerts!*

Then a frown crossed Rachel's face. She had forgotten one very important factor: her father.

Dad is not going to like this, she thought. *I already know what he'll say: "Sorry, Rachel, but you're just not old enough to go to a concert like this." This is going to be awful. Everybody will be there—except for me!*

Determination flickered in Rachel's eyes. *Unless I can prove to Dad that I* am *mature enough,* she realized. *If I don't ask him right away—if I spend every day before the concert proving that I'm not a little kid anymore— then maybe he'll see my side. I mean, this is a once-in-a-lifetime opportunity. I'm sure that all my friends will get to go. And besides, Dad knows Brody! He's known*

Brody's family for years through church.

Rachel started scribbling a list on the back cover of her notebook: *Fold the laundry. Help Robbie pick up his toys. Make my bed every day. Put away the clean dishes without being asked.*

As she wrote, Rachel thought of even more ways that she could help around the house—just like a responsible adult would. And she also realized that even though she'd always tried to take care of Robbie as much as she could, there was still more that she could do. That would make everybody's lives easier . . . and maybe show her dad, once and for all, that she wasn't a little girl anymore.

Near the end of the school day a bitter wind kicked up, and small icy chunks of snow began to fall. Rachel and Taylor had to wrap their scarves around their faces to keep out the cold, which meant that they couldn't chat like they usually did when they walked home from school together. When she finally made it into her house, Rachel breathed a sigh of relief as the comforting warmth enveloped her.

"Cocoa's on the stove," Grandma Nellie said in a hushed voice as she helped Rachel unwrap her frozen scarf. "Your dad's going to be pulling a double tonight, so he's resting before he heads out. Robbie's watching a video, if you have any interest in that one with the dancing ducks."

Rachel giggled. "Maybe next time," she replied. "I think I'll start my homework."

But halfway to her bedroom, Rachel stopped. If her dad was going to plow for a double shift, that meant he'd be eating dinner on the road. And sometimes, if the snow was very heavy, he had trouble finding a drive-through that was still open. *I could make him dinner,* she realized. *I could pack an awesome dinner that he could take with him tonight!*

Rachel went right to the kitchen and started a fresh pot of coffee. Then she scoured the pantry for something tasty and filling for her dad's dinner. *Chicken soup—perfect!* she thought. *And I could make a couple sandwiches, too. Maybe a banana . . . and an apple . . . and definitely a brownie. . . .*

Rachel opened a can of chicken soup and dumped it into a bowl. Then she microwaved it for two minutes so that it would be nice and hot. When she carefully poured the soup into a thermos, though, Rachel frowned. *That's a whole can of soup?* she wondered. *It doesn't look like enough. Maybe I should give him two.*

Rachel warmed up another can of soup and added it to the thermos. Then she made some sandwiches and placed the rest of the food in a paper grocery bag. By the time she was finished, the coffee was ready, so Rachel poured it into a second thermos and added a spoonful of sugar, just the way her dad liked it. When Mr. Wilson came into the kitchen a few minutes later wearing his warmest flannel shirt, Rachel was ready for him.

"Don't forget your dinner!" she said proudly as she handed her dad the bag.

He looked surprised. "What's this?" he asked.

"I wanted to make sure you had something good to eat tonight," Rachel explained. "There's soup and sandwiches, some fruit, a brownie . . . and coffee. With sugar."

Mr. Wilson pulled Rachel into a hug. "Thanks a lot, kiddo," he said. "That was very considerate of you." He glanced out the window, where large fluffy flakes were swirling wildly. "Gonna be a long night, I think. We might get two feet—or more. But this great dinner will make it easier to handle."

"Drive safely, Dad," Rachel said as she stepped up on her tiptoes to give him a kiss. "I love you!"

"Love you, too," he replied with a big smile.

Rachel watched her dad walk into the storm. She wished that he didn't have to go, but at least he'd have something warm to eat and drink for the long night ahead.

Rachel woke up the next morning to a great surprise: a snow day! She cheered—quietly, of course, so that she wouldn't wake her dad—and got dressed as fast as she could. After she finished eating breakfast, Rachel decided to tackle the dishes. Then maybe she and Taylor could take Robbie sledding.

Rachel blitzed through the dishes and loaded the dishwasher in just a few minutes. There were only a few things she had to wash by hand—the oatmeal pot and the two thermoses she had packed for her dad. But to Rachel's surprise, the soup one was still full.

Why didn't Dad eat the soup I made him? she wondered. Rachel sniffed it. The soup smelled fine. It was still warm, even. Chicken noodle was her dad's favorite. She had made the right flavor, right? She dug one of the empty cans out of the recycle bin and saw that the label read CONDENSED. Somehow, she hadn't noticed it the night before.

"Grandma Nellie?" Rachel asked as she wandered into the living room. "What does 'condensed' mean? On a can of soup?"

Grandma Nellie glanced up from her scrapbook page. "Oh, that just means it's concentrated. You have to add water before you eat it."

"You do?" Rachel asked with a sinking feeling.

Grandma Nellie nodded. "Otherwise, it's too salty and thick to eat."

"Oh," Rachel said. "Okay. Thanks."

But as she walked back into the kitchen, Rachel was so mad at herself that she felt like kicking the empty can across the floor. *That was so dumb,* she thought. *Why didn't I read the directions on the label? I'm sure Dad really loved having a big thermos full of nasty salty soup that was too goopy to eat! So much for acting like a responsible adult!*

Rachel tried to forget about her mistake while she and Taylor played in the snow with Robbie for most of the afternoon. When they went inside to warm up, Rachel decided to check her LifeChat page to see how her other friends were spending the snow day. The posts were flying across the screen so fast that Rachel knew something big must've happened.

Grace Everett: Not a rumor!!!

Nevaeh Fry: but who told u?

Amber Jones: I heard it 2

Charlotte Chang: I heard it from Jessie so u know it's true

"T, you better check this out," Rachel called as she stared at her computer.

Taylor leaned over Rachel's shoulder and read all the posts. "What's going on?" she asked excitedly.

"Don't know yet," Rachel replied as her fingers flew across the keyboard. "Let's find out!"

Rachel Wilson: just logged on. What's up??

Charlotte Chang: OMG, rach, BIG BIG BIG news

Rachel Wilson: spill!

Becca Morrison: there is going 2 be a dance after brody's concert!

Nevaeh Fry: maybe. we don't know 4 sure

Amber Jones: i heard it from madison. she should know, she is bff with student council pres

Giada Lough: me too. there was a student council mtg after school yesterday

Giada Lough: it was supposed to be announced today but school got canceled

Giada Lough: they will tell us tmrw

Amber Jones: this is the best part—madison said that jessie emailed brody to invite him & his secret crush!

Grace Everett: TO THE DANCE?!?!?!

Amber Jones: YES!!!

Taylor gasped. "Rachel! Brody is going to be at the Valentine's dance! Are you freaking out?"

"No." Rachel laughed. "I mean, he *might* be at the dance. *If* there's even going to be a dance. I'll believe it when I hear Ms. Gutierrez say it in homeroom announcements."

"Don't be like that," Taylor replied. "Come on, aren't you excited? Just a little?"

"But what's the point of getting excited if it might not even happen?" Rachel asked. She remembered how thrilled she was to listen to "Secret Crush"— and how terrible she'd felt when she realized that practically every single girl at school wanted to be Brody's crush too. "You'll just feel more disappointed later."

"But Archer is the most boring place in the world. Nothing exciting ever happens here . . . until *now* . . . and I want to enjoy it! And you should too!" Taylor replied. "Here, let me play with your hair. It would look so awesome with a purple streak in the front, especially if you pull it back. We could use that temporary hair spray stuff. But would your dad let you do that? Or I guess maybe we should figure out what to wear first? I think we should both wear red for Valentine's Day. You have a red tunic in your closet somewhere, right . . . ?"

Rachel grinned in spite of herself and watched as her best friend started rummaging through her closet. Taylor's enthusiasm was contagious, as usual. Rachel knew that convincing her dad to let her go to the dance—if it actually happened—wasn't going to be easy. But she vowed to herself right then and there that, no matter what, she'd figure out a way to make her dad let her go.

chapter 5

TAYLOR HAD AN ORTHODONTIST APPOINTMENT
the next morning, so Rachel didn't see her best friend
until lunchtime.

"Told you so! Told you so! Told you so!" Taylor cried
as she patted the chair next to her. She always sounded a
little different after she got her braces tightened. "Here, I
saved you a seat. So? Are you excited now?"

"Excited?" Rachel repeated. She pretended to look
confused. "About what? Oh, the dance?"

Taylor's eyes grew wide. "Of course about the dance!"
she said. "Don't tell me that you forgot about it. I was sure
you'd be flipping out—"

"I'm just messing with you," Rachel interrupted,
grinning at Taylor.

"So the craziest thing happened in science today,"
Taylor said. "Brian asked Emily to go to the dance with

him! I thought I was going to fall off my chair! And then, like, ten minutes later, Colin asked Samantha."

"In my English class, Lauren asked Henry," Rachel said.

Taylor's mouth dropped open. "*Lauren* and *Henry!*" she exclaimed. "I never would have guessed. That's crazy."

"It's kind of weird, huh?" Rachel asked. "I mean, usually nobody even goes to the dances at school. And now, all of a sudden, *everybody* wants to go. And with a date, too! That never happens."

"What never happens?" the girls' friend Shane Allen asked as he sat down across from them.

"Hey, Shane," Taylor said. "We were just talking about the Valentine's dance."

Shane rolled his eyes a little. "Yeah, you and the rest of the school," he said.

"I know, right?" Rachel exclaimed. "It's weird, huh? And now all these people are going together—like as a date!"

"Yup," Shane said through a mouthful of spaghetti. He paused for a minute to finish chewing. "Totally weird. I don't know—I hope some people go by themselves. It would be really awkward to be the only person there without a date."

"*Totally* awkward," Rachel repeated emphatically. She started wondering (again) if anyone would ask her to the dance. She kind of hoped not. After all, if Brody was going to be there—and if, by some crazy long shot, he actually *liked* her—then Rachel didn't want to be stuck with a date. Just since homeroom, she had imagined the dance about a hundred times. *The gym will be dim, with little twinkly lights everywhere. Maybe I'll be standing off to the side with Taylor, and then suddenly I'll see Brody walking toward me. But I won't be sure, and I won't want to stare at him, but every time I glance that way—there he is. With that smile that reaches all the way to his eyes, and he's going to be looking right at me, and then he'll say, "Rachel, do you want to dance?" And instead of being all nervous, I'll just smile and say, "Sure," like it's no big deal, and follow him onto the dance floor and—*

Suddenly Rachel realized that Shane and Taylor had stopped talking. They were both staring at her. "Um, what?" she said, biting her lip. "Sorry, I—did you say something?"

Shane fidgeted with his fork. "Yeah, I just—no big deal, but I asked if you wanted to go to the dance with me? As friends. That way we won't be the only ones without a date."

A feeling of dread settled over Rachel. How could she say no? Shane was such a nice guy. She really didn't want to hurt his feelings. But Brody's face flashed through her mind, and she started to stammer, "Um—I don't—"

"Actually, I'd love to go with you," Taylor said to Shane, rescuing Rachel just in time. "You know, Rachel might not even be allowed to go to the dance, and I was worried that I wouldn't have anyone to hang out with. I think we'll have an awesome time!"

Rachel flashed Taylor a grateful smile.

"Okay, Taylor," Shane said. "Sounds great."

But Shane's smile didn't seem quite genuine, and Rachel knew that he could tell that she was going to say no. She didn't want Shane to feel totally rejected.

"Shane, ordinarily I would definitely go with you," Rachel said quickly. "It's just that—well, this is top secret so don't tell anyone, but . . . I'm kind of hoping to go to the dance with Brody."

Shane looked shocked. "Brody?" he repeated. "You and *Brody*?"

Rachel was stung. She didn't know what to say. *Is it*

really that hard to believe? she thought.

But Shane quickly corrected himself. "I'm just surprised because I had no idea that you even knew Brody," he continued.

Rachel nodded. "Yeah, we've been in our church choir for years. I mean, we *were* in it—before Brody moved to California."

"You sing?" Now Shane looked even more surprised. "I didn't know that. How come you're not in glee club?"

"Because—actually, never mind. It's not important. Besides, I get to sing a lot at church," Rachel replied.

"And you and Brody are . . . friends?" Shane asked.

Rachel shrugged. "I guess. I mean, we were friendly. But just between us—" she leaned forward and lowered her voice—"I've had a crush on him forever. I know it's probably not going to matter—"

"Wait a minute," Shane said. "Do you think that *you're* Brody's secret crush?"

Rachel didn't say anything, but the pink blush creeping over her face answered Shane's question.

"Wow, Rach, I honestly had no idea that you like Brody. That's so . . . you know what? I really hope that Brody likes you, too. Maybe you *are* his secret crush!" Shane said genuinely—and loudly. At least ten people nearby turned to stare at them! Rachel wished that she could dive under the cafeteria table and never be seen again. She bent down and rummaged around in her backpack like there was a secret treasure hidden there.

"Shane!" Taylor hissed. "Shut up!"

Shane's eyes grew wide. "Oops, sorry, that was kind of loud," he said in a quieter voice.

"I want to die," Rachel moaned in a half whisper from under the table. "I'm so embarrassed."

"Rach, don't even worry about it," Taylor said. "Come up. Nobody's even looking over here anymore. Honestly, I don't think that anyone was even paying attention."

"Then why were they all *staring* at me?" Rachel demanded.

"Nobody was staring. They just kind of . . . looked in this direction for a second," Taylor replied, but Rachel didn't completely believe her. She wanted to, though.

"You really think so?" Rachel asked.

"Definitely," Taylor said firmly.

She must have kicked Shane under the table, because he jumped and quickly said, "Yeah, I mean, I wasn't *that* loud. Besides, practically every girl in this school is in *love* with Brody. Nobody's going to care about your crush, you know? It would probably be a bigger deal if you *didn't* like him!"

"I hope you're right," Rachel said as the bell rang, feeling a little better. She had never been so glad about the end of lunch period before. As Rachel threw away her trash, she thought about what Shane had said. It was true that all the girls were acting kind of crazy about Brody right now. If anything, Rachel figured, Shane's big announcement would make her fit right in.

Then, as she and Taylor walked into the hallway, Colin Mercer looked right at Rachel, grinned, and belted out a line from "Secret Crush." Everyone around them cracked up, like they usually did when Colin started messing around. Stunned, Rachel blinked back tears of embarrassment.

"Aw, Rach, don't," Taylor said softly. "Everybody's laughing at *Colin*, not you. I really don't think anyone will care about your crush. Shane's right. A year ago, it might have been gossip-worthy, but not when so many other girls are crushing on Brody too."

"I just—I didn't want anybody to know," Rachel

replied. "And now the whole school does. What if somebody tells Brody?"

"What would they say?" Taylor asked. "'Hey, Brody, every single girl at school is crazy about you, especially that Rachel Wilson!'" Taylor shook her head. "Not gonna happen. Besides, it seems like Brody's not really in touch with anybody these days. He's too busy. So it could be worse."

Rachel nodded slowly. "You're right. Thanks, Taylor," she said.

"No problem," said Taylor. "Trust me, by seventh period no one is even going to care—or remember."

For a few hours, Rachel almost believed her. But when she went to her locker after school, Rachel found a huge surprise.

Tammy Hemmings was waiting for her.

Oh man, Rachel thought as she automatically slowed down. *Why is Tammy standing at my locker?*

Even as the question formed in Rachel's mind, she figured out the answer. Tammy must have heard about her crush, just like everybody else at school. *What am I even going to say to her?* Rachel wondered wildly. *She's probably going to tell me to stay away from Brody or—*

"Hey," Tammy said. She shifted her weight from one leg to the other. "You're Rachel, right?"

Rachel hesitated for a moment before she spoke. "Yeah," she finally replied. "Um, hi."

"Hey," Tammy said again. She smiled a little and glanced, briefly, at the floor. Suddenly, Rachel realized that Tammy felt about as awkward as she did. "So . . . about Brody . . ."

"So you heard about that," Rachel said.

Tammy nodded. "Listen, I don't blame you. He is *so* cute. But there was—well—there was something I was kind of curious about. Can I ask you a question?"

"I guess," Rachel replied. "I mean, sure."

"I was just wondering . . . what makes you think that 'Secret Crush' is about you?" Tammy asked.

"Oh," Rachel said. "Well, it was that line about making music together. You know the one?"

Tammy nodded.

"Brody and I sang together in our church choir," Rachel explained. She shrugged. "That's all. It probably doesn't mean anything."

"I didn't know that Brody was in a church choir, too," Tammy said. "I thought he was just in glee club. Maybe you're right. Maybe that line *is* about choir and not glee."

Rachel felt a little hope stirring inside her heart, but tried to ignore it.

"So, what do you think about the L-O-L line?" Tammy continued. "Did you and Brody joke around a lot in choir?"

"No," Rachel admitted. "Like, never. Did you guys? In glee club?"

"Yeah," Tammy said. "Practically after every rehearsal."

"Oh," Rachel said. "So . . . that's probably it, then. That's probably the clue." She tried to act like it was no big deal, but the smile she forced across her face was hardly convincing.

"Who knows," Tammy said with a shrug. "Whatever the clue is, it's definitely not easy to figure out. But good luck, Rachel. If I'm not Brody's crush . . . then I hope it's you."

"Me too," Rachel said. "Wait, that didn't sound right."

Tammy's laugh, as beautiful as her singing voice, rang through the hallway. "No worries," she assured Rachel. "I know what you meant. See ya."

"See ya," Rachel repeated. She opened her locker

and started loading her backpack, oblivious to everyone else in the hallway. *Tammy was just trying to be nice,* Rachel thought, forcing herself to face the truth. *Because, sure, the music line could be about choir or glee club. But the LOL part—that's got to be all about her.*

And not me.

WHEN RACHEL GOT HOME, SHE WENT STRAIGHT
to Grandma Nellie's scrapbooking cupboard. "Grandma Nellie?" she called. "Can I take some more of your supplies?"

"Of course, honey," Grandma Nellie replied. "Anything you want. Did you decide to give scrapbooking a try?"

"Yep," Rachel said as she loaded up on paper, glue, and ribbon. "I worked on it a little bit already the other night. Now I have some more pages I want to add."

"Good for you, Rachel! I bet it will look great," Grandma Nellie said. "Have fun!"

In her room Rachel started playing *Songs from My Heart* as she arranged the supplies on her desk. Then she used her hole punch to make a series of holes around the edge of a new scrapbook page. After weaving a pretty piece of crimson ribbon through the holes, Rachel pulled out a sheet of the lined pink paper and was ready to start writing.

The most embarrassing choir practice ever turned out to be the best. It was last winter, and practically the whole town had the flu. When I got to practice, I was the only soprano. So whenever I sang the soprano part, it was like a giant solo. So if I hit a wrong note, everybody would know that it was me.

At first my voice was small and squeaky, like a mouse. Halfway through the song Mr. Jenkins stopped us. I knew he wasn't going to be happy, and it was all my fault.

But instead, he started talking about why we sing at church. He talked about how singing was a miracle, and if you managed to lose yourself in it, it was beautiful no matter what.

For the next song, I just closed my eyes and pretended that I was home alone, singing where nobody could hear me. And it worked! I just lost myself in it and it felt great.

When the song ended, I was a little bit dizzy and breathless, but I didn't even care. And then—this had never happened before—everybody started clapping and cheering. For me!! Mr. Jenkins was smiling so big.

Then, after practice, Brody came up to me. I had just started noticing how incredibly cute he is, which made me feel a little nervous around him. Brody said, "Rachel! That was amazing! I didn't know you could sing like that!" And then Brody asked me why I wasn't in glee club at school.

I wanted to tell him why not—that I wasn't allowed to even try out—but I couldn't. The last thing I wanted was for Brody to think my dad was crazy strict. Not too many people would understand how much things had changed after Mom left.

So I just said, "Oh, I'm kind of busy during the week," like it was no big deal.

"You have to join glee," Brody said. He was totally serious. "I'll talk to Mrs. Serang about a special audition, if you want. Seriously, Rachel, we need you!"

I had to keep saying "No, that's okay," and I felt really bad . . . like I was hurting his feelings. He finally let it go and said, "I'll see you later, Rachel."

It meant so much to me that he thought I was good enough to be in glee club with him . . . but of course I couldn't tell him that, either.

Rachel put down her pen. *If only Brody and I had been in glee club together too,* she thought sadly. *We could've hung out more. Gotten to know each other better. And maybe I'd be his secret crush. Maybe the message in the song would make more sense.*

She carefully glued the pink paper with her writing on it at the center of the new page with the ribbon. Then, using some of the letter stencils that she had borrowed from Grandma Nellie, she traced and cut out eight letters from felt. When she was finished, she carefully pasted the letters at the top of the page, above the entry she had written.

MIRACLES.

Satisfied, Rachel moved the scrapbook page over to an empty spot on her dresser so the glue could dry. Then she returned to her desk and turned on her computer to check her e-mail. To her surprise, she had an e-mail from Brody himself!

From: the_real_brody@brodywarner.com

To: friends [list]

Date: February 6

Subject: Party @ Chocolate Bar

Hey guys! Not too long till I'm back in town, and I can't wait! I'll be flying in next Thursday, a couple days before the concert, and it would be awesome to hang out with you guys that night before things get all crazy. My team booked the Chocolate Bar for a private event and you're all invited. It's at six p.m. and there's gonna be an unlimited chocolate fountain (AWESOME). I really hope you can come . . . it wouldn't be the same without you.

BRODY

Just seeing Brody's name appear in her in-box made Rachel's heart start pounding. A private party at the Chocolate Bar? With *Brody*?! It sounded too good to be true. Hannah Schwartz had her bat mitzvah party at the Chocolate Bar, and it had been the most sophisticated, elegant evening of Rachel's life. Not to mention, all the chocolate treats were delicious. Rachel imagined sitting next to Brody on one of the velvet-covered couches, telling him about everything that was going on in church choir—

Then Rachel stopped herself. *Who am I kidding?* she thought.

Like Dad would even let me go.

Rachel glanced at the scrapbook page she had just made. Miracles. It looked like she was going to need a miracle to be allowed to go to Brody's party.

Rachel felt her eyes fill up with tears. She knew it wasn't very grown-up to cry, but she couldn't help it. Sometimes it was hard to act like everything was going to be okay, when deep down she knew it probably wasn't going to be.

How much more of my life am I going to miss because of Dad's rules? Rachel wondered. *I have to find a way to make him trust me. Otherwise . . .*

A knock at the door interrupted Rachel's thoughts. "Come in," she called.

It was Grandma Nellie, carrying a bowl of popcorn and a mug of steaming cider. "I noticed you were so busy scrapbooking that you forgot to have a snack," she said. "Can't say I blame you. I've felt the same way!"

"Thanks—that smells good," Rachel replied in a dull voice.

Grandma Nellie could tell right away that something was wrong. "You okay, sweet pea?" she asked.

Rachel didn't know where to begin. "Do you think I act mature?" she asked.

"Mature?" Grandma Nellie repeated. "What do you mean?"

"Like . . . not like a little kid anymore," Rachel tried to explain. "Like somebody who's old enough to go to a concert. Or a dance. Or a party on a school night."

Grandma Nellie's eyes brightened. "Well, which is it, honey? A concert or a dance or a party on a school night?"

Rachel couldn't help smiling back. "Grandma Nellie, it's all three!" she said. And then the words came tumbling out as Rachel told Grandma Nellie all about Brody's big concert, the Valentine's Day dance, and the private party at the Chocolate Bar.

"And your whole class is invited?" Grandma Nellie asked. "And the concert tickets are free?"

Rachel nodded.

"Oh, Rachel, you *have* to go!" Grandma Nellie said at once, clapping her hands enthusiastically. "What an experience! And Brody Warner is such a nice boy. His mother used to drive me to my doctor appointments after I broke my ankle. The Warners are good people, there's no doubt about that."

"But . . . what about Dad?" Rachel asked.

Grandma Nellie waved her hand in the air dismissively. "Don't worry about your father. Tell you what—there isn't supposed to be any snow tomorrow, so he'll definitely be home for dinner. We'll make a special meal . . . maybe chicken stew? And you can make his favorite dessert—an apple pie! We'll have a lovely family night and then, after dinner, you can ask permission. And I'll be right there to help you convince him. Not that I think he'll need it, sweetheart."

"Really?" Rachel gasped. She leaped up and threw her arms around Grandma Nellie. "Thank you,

Grandma Nellie! You're the best!"

"Oh, honey, no need to thank me," Grandma Nellie replied as she hugged Rachel back. Then, smiling, she pushed Rachel's hair back from her face. "You really are growing into such a lovely young woman. So mature and responsible. Don't think I don't know how much you do around here . . . for everybody. And life is getting so exciting for you. I can't wait to see what happens next!"

"Me neither," Rachel said. Grandma Nellie's enthusiasm was infectious, just like Taylor's. Rachel could hardly believe how hopeful she suddenly felt. Even if Rachel couldn't convince her dad to let her go to all the upcoming events, he would surely listen to Grandma Nellie.

chapter 7

"WE'RE HOME!" MR. WILSON CALLED OUT THE NEXT night as he walked through the door, carrying Robbie on his shoulders.

"Hey, Dad!" Rachel exclaimed as she poked her head out of the kitchen. She was wearing one of Grandma Nellie's aprons. "I feel like I've barely seen you for days."

"Me too, kiddo," Mr. Wilson said, smiling at Rachel. "We've had a pretty rough winter so far. It's good for the bank account, but bad for family time. Luckily, we should have clear weather for the rest of the weekend, at least." Then he paused and sniffed the air. "Wow, what smells so delicious?"

"I can't tell you," Rachel said mysteriously. "And don't come into the kitchen until I say so!"

Leaving her dad in the entryway, Rachel hurried back to the stove. "He's home," she said to Grandma Nellie.

"How much longer until dinner?"

Grandma Nellie lifted the lid off the pot and tasted the broth. "The stew is ready," she replied. "And it's delicious!"

"I'm worried about the pie," Rachel said anxiously. "What if the crust is dry? Or the apples are mushy?"

"The pie is going to be perfect," Grandma Nellie declared. "You did a great job on it, and I should know. I'm a pie expert, after all."

Rachel smiled at her grandmother, but she still looked a little worried.

Fortunately, all of the food was delicious, and everyone had seconds of the savory chicken stew—even Robbie. And when Rachel served up big slabs of pie crowned with creamy vanilla ice cream, she was relieved to see that Grandma Nellie was right: The pie was perfect! The Wilsons had such a nice dinner that it was twenty minutes past Robbie's bedtime before Mr. Wilson glanced at his watch.

"Whoa, buddy," he exclaimed. "Bedtime for you!"

Robbie opened his mouth like he wanted to argue, but a big yawn escaped instead. Everyone else laughed as Grandma Nellie helped him out of his booster seat.

"I'll handle bedtime tonight," she said. "Go give Daddy a big hug and kiss, Robbie."

"I'll get started on the dishes," Rachel said as she began stacking the plates.

"I can do it," Mr. Wilson said. He followed her into the kitchen.

"No way, Dad. I got it," Rachel told him.

Mr. Wilson stood in the doorway for a moment before he said, "Well, I can put away the leftovers, at least. So what's going on at school these days?"

"The usual," Rachel replied. "Um, I got a ninety-two on my math test."

"Great job!" Mr. Wilson told her. "But what happened to the other eight points?"

"Ha-ha," Rachel replied.

"I'm just giving you a hard time," her dad said. "You know I'm proud of you, Rach. But it's my dad-job to push you to do better."

How many times had Rachel heard that speech? But instead of sighing or rolling her eyes, she just said, "I know, Dad. I'll try harder."

"That's all I ask," Mr. Wilson said.

They finished tidying the kitchen in silence until Grandma Nellie joined them. "He sleeps!" she joked. "Carl, do you want some coffee? Another piece of pie, perhaps?"

"Coffee would be great," he said.

"You go have a seat in the living room and Rachel and I will be right out," Grandma Nellie said, with a sly wink at Rachel.

Rachel's heart was pounding when she brought her dad a steaming cup of coffee a few minutes later. She tried to smile normally as she placed it on a coaster in front of him.

"Thanks, Rachel," her dad said, without looking up from the newspaper.

Rachel hated to interrupt him—but she didn't think she could wait another minute to ask him about the party. "Um, Dad?" she began. "Do you remember Brody Warner? From church?"

"Sure, he's the big rock star now, right?"

"Something like that," Rachel said as Grandma Nellie sat in the armchair across from them. "Well, he's going to be in town next week, and he's having a party at the Chocolate Bar on Thursday."

That got Mr. Wilson's attention. He folded the paper and put it on the table—but said nothing.

"So . . . I was hoping I could go," said Rachel. "It's at six o'clock, so I'd have plenty of time to get my homework done before it starts. And I'm sure it will be over by eight."

Mr. Wilson still didn't respond.

"But I could leave early," Rachel said in a rush. "At seven thirty. Or seven. Whenever you want me to."

"I'd be happy to pick her up," Grandma Nellie chimed in.

"I don't think that's a good idea," Mr. Wilson finally said.

"Grandma Nellie picking me up?" Rachel asked in confusion. "Or leaving early?"

Mr. Wilson shook his head. "No, the *party* isn't a good idea," he said. "For one thing, Rachel, Thursday is a school night. I'm surprised you *even* asked. You know the rule: No socializing on school nights."

"But, Dad—" Rachel began.

"For another thing, Thursdays are family night," Mr. Wilson continued. "I go to a lot of trouble finding someone to cover for me on Thursdays so that there's at least *one* night a week that we can all enjoy dinner as a family. And wasn't that nice tonight? Didn't we all have a good time?"

"Yes, but—"

"No buts, Rachel," Mr. Wilson said firmly. "My decision is final."

Rachel shot a desperate glance at Grandma Nellie.

"Carl, wait a minute," Grandma Nellie spoke up. "Let's hear what else Rachel has to say."

Rachel took a deep breath. This was her big chance. "It's just—Dad, this party is really, really important to me," she said. "Brody hasn't been home since last summer, and I didn't even see him then because I had to miss his pool party. And all my friends are going to be there! I just—"

"*All* your friends?" Mr. Wilson repeated skeptically. "I find that a little hard to believe. I can't think of a single parent who would let their child attend a party at a *bar*. On a school night."

Rachel's face burned with frustration. "Dad! It's not a bar or a club or anything. It's, like, a café that serves only desserts. Like a fancy bakery. Besides, I've already been there—it's where Hannah had her bat mitzvah party!"

"But that wasn't a school night," Mr. Wilson reminded her.

"Okay," Rachel said. "Is that the only problem? Because on Valentine's Day—that's a Saturday—there's going to be a dance at school, and before—"

"Surely a school dance won't be a problem, Carl," Grandma Nellie interrupted Rachel.

Rachel glanced over at her, confused. Didn't Grandma Nellie understand that she was about to ask permission to go to the concert, too?

Or maybe, Rachel suddenly realized, she did. And maybe Grandma Nellie had a very good reason for wanting Rachel to keep quiet about the concert.

"A dance?" Mr. Wilson repeated. "I suppose that would be all right, since it's a school function. And on a Saturday, instead of a weeknight."

"Thanks, Dad," Rachel said stiffly. "I have a little more reading to do before Monday."

Mr. Wilson nodded as he reached for the newspaper. "Your pie was great, Rachel," he said. "Thanks again."

Back in her room, Rachel stretched out on her bed and stared at the ceiling. She wasn't entirely sure what had just happened. Somehow going to the dance was fine, but the party wasn't? And why had Grandma Nellie stopped her from mentioning the concert?

A few minutes later, Rachel heard Grandma Nellie's soft knock at the door. She entered the room with a shopping bag in her hands.

"I got these for you today," Grandma Nellie said. "I thought it was time you had some of your very own scrapbooking supplies—you know, things that will reflect you and your interests."

Rachel peeked inside the bag and found a hole punch in the shape of musical notes and a clef-shaped stamp. The shimmery paper was in her favorite shade of lavender. There was also a pack of seven glitter-gel pens and a pad of rainbow-colored lined paper for writing more journal-style entries.

"Thanks, Grandma Nellie," Rachel said. "These are great."

But even though Rachel meant every word, there was a flatness in her voice that made Grandma Nellie sigh. The bed creaked as Grandma Nellie sat next to Rachel. "Want to talk about it?"

"It's a bakery!" Rachel exclaimed, more loudly than she intended. "They sell fancy desserts and stuff! Gourmet hot chocolate! *And he already let me go to a party there before!* So why is he acting like it's some totally inappropriate nightclub or something? Sometimes I think he *likes* to say no for no good reason!"

"I don't think that's what's going on," Grandma Nellie said in a soothing voice. "I know it's hard to understand this, Rachel, but your father is just doing what he thinks is right. It's hard for him that he has to make decisions on his own, and I think he just ends up being too cautious sometimes."

"Can't you talk to him?" Rachel asked. "You weren't so strict with Dad when he was my age, were you?"

Grandma Nellie frowned as she tried to remember. "I don't *think* I was . . . ," she began. "But honey, when I moved in, I promised your dad that I would support the decisions he made for you and Robbie. I'm sorry that I couldn't intervene more tonight, but it was very clear that his mind was made up."

"So why didn't you want me to ask him about the concert?" asked Rachel.

"Because I knew that he was going to say no," Grandma Nellie said. "You know he doesn't like to change his mind once he's made a decision. He's stubborn that way . . . like me. And, frankly, Rachel, I think you should go to the concert. So I'd rather you *not* ask and *not* get a firm no from your dad."

"That makes me feel worse," Rachel said quietly. "I don't want to lie to Dad."

"Look at it this way," Grandma Nellie said. "Whenever your dad isn't home, I'm the one who's responsible for you. And *I* would give you permission to go. Okay?"

"I still feel like a liar."

"Oh, sweetie, *don't*," Grandma Nellie said at once.

"I'll try to find a time to talk to him privately this week and see if I can't convince him to give you a little more freedom. You know, it's not always easy to watch your children grow up. Take it from me, I know. And your father might just need a little help with it."

"If you could talk to him, that would be great," Rachel said. "I just . . . I don't want to go behind his back or anything. I guess I should just be grateful that he said I could go to the dance."

"And I'm going to do my best to get you to that concert, too," promised Grandma Nellie. She stood up and walked over to the door. "Hang in there, peach pie. Nobody said that growing up would be easy."

"Yeah . . . but don't you think it could be *easier?*" Rachel asked.

Grandma Nellie laughed as she left the room, making Rachel smile. But once Rachel was alone again, the smile disappeared from her face. What Grandma Nellie had said made sense to Rachel . . . kind of. But there was still a deep, unsettled feeling nagging at her. It was the same kind of feeling she sometimes got when she knew she wasn't making the right decision—like that time in sixth grade when a bunch of Rachel's friends had started shutting out Jenna Ferguson, and Rachel had just gone along with it. Then, in church one Sunday, Rachel had listened to a sermon about loving thy neighbor, and everything just *clicked*. Suddenly, Rachel realized that even though she hadn't done anything mean to Jenna, she hadn't exactly been nice to her either. And that was just as bad. Tonight, sitting alone in her bedroom, Rachel felt that squirming discomfort again. It was the knowledge that she had a clear choice to make . . . and she was tempted to make the wrong one.

Lying to my dad is not how I want to go to the concert, she thought. *It would only prove that I'm really not mature.*

Rachel knew, without a doubt, that she had to tell her dad about the concert. And she also knew that if she did that, she would need to convince him to let her go.

The only question was: how?

RACHEL HAD A LOT OF TROUBLE CONCENTRATING at school the following week. Every time her friends mentioned Brody's upcoming party at the Chocolate Bar, she had to force a smile so nobody could tell how disappointed she was. Rachel wasn't alone—lots of kids who didn't know Brody hadn't been invited—but that didn't make it any easier for Rachel to know that she *could've* gone to the party.

But Rachel wasn't entirely miserable. By Thursday, the day of the party, Rachel found herself caught up in all the excitement anyway. After all, even though she wouldn't be seeing Brody tonight, she'd be seeing him soon enough! As she sat in math class after lunch, Rachel wondered, *Is Brody still on the plane? Has the plane landed yet? Will he go straight to his old house? Or check out the arena? Or maybe he'll even surprise everybody by coming to school!*

That didn't happen, but Rachel didn't really expect it to. After all, Brody couldn't exactly walk anywhere anymore without being mobbed by crazy fans. While Rachel and Taylor walked home from school, Rachel kept scanning the cars that passed them, just in case Brody happened to be in one. Somehow just knowing that he was back in Archer made Rachel feel tingly all over. It had been a long time since she had daydreamed about running into Brody around town—and now the possibility that she might see him at any moment made living in Archer a lot more exciting than it had been just a day ago.

That afternoon, even though Rachel hadn't quite finished her homework, Grandma Nellie gave her permission to go over to Taylor's house. Rachel had never seen Taylor look quite so excited. Her cheeks were pink before she put on any makeup, and even her eyes seemed more sparkly than usual.

"What should we do first?" Rachel asked. "Hair or nails?"

Taylor bit her lip as she thought about it. "Nails, I guess," she replied. "But only if you'll do my hair. Then my nails can dry before I have to get dressed."

"Of course I'll do your hair!" Rachel said with a laugh.

"That's why I'm here. So what color nail polish are you thinking about?" Rachel didn't know a whole lot about makeup, since she wasn't allowed to wear any, but when she'd turned twelve her dad gave her permission to start wearing nail polish. She had quite a collection of polishes now, and she had brought some of her favorites over in case Taylor wanted to borrow any of them. "I've narrowed it down to these two," Taylor said, showing Rachel a midnight-blue polish and a sparkly gold one. "What do you think?"

"I like the sparkles," Rachel said. "But I think the blue will look better with your top. Oh, I know!"

Rachel dug around in her bag and pulled out a clear polish with specks of silver glitter. "How about the blue polish with a coat of this on top?"

"Perfect!" Taylor squealed. "Thanks, Rach!" She laid her hands flat on the desk as Rachel shook the blue polish in her palm. When she started painting Taylor's nails, Rachel concentrated so hard that she forgot to talk.

"So . . . ," Taylor began. "Something kind of exciting happened last night."

The way that Taylor's voice trembled a little made Rachel look up right away. "Tell me," she ordered.

"Shane texted me!" Taylor exclaimed. "He's never done that before!"

That's the exciting news? Rachel thought. A text message didn't seem like a huge deal to her . . . unless there was something special *about* the message. "What did he say?"

"He asked me to go to the party with him tonight!"

There was something surprising about Taylor's reaction—something that Rachel hadn't expected. She'd been sitting right there when Shane and Taylor agreed to go to the dance together as friends. It had been as basic and boring as asking somebody when the history project was due. But this . . . this was different.

"So you guys are going to the party together too?" Rachel asked.

Taylor nodded as the smile on her face grew even larger.

"Taylor! You *like* him!" Rachel exclaimed. "Why didn't you tell me? Aaaah! I'm so excited for you! You and Shane—I can't believe it!"

"I can't either!" Taylor shrieked. "It's just . . . we've kind of been talking more since last week, and you know, Rach, he's really funny."

"I know."

"No, I mean, like, *really* funny," Taylor emphasized. "And he's really into computers and technology, which is so cool. He knows a ton about websites and is even writing his own app."

"Seriously?" Rachel asked, impressed.

"I know!" Taylor gushed. "And I can't believe I didn't realize this before, but Rach . . . isn't he so incredibly cute?"

Shane? Incredibly cute? Rachel thought about it for a moment. Shane was a pretty good-looking guy, with dark brown hair that perfectly matched his eyes, and a quick, sly smile. But if Brody set the bar for "incredibly cute," then no, Shane wouldn't qualify. *But it doesn't matter if you think he's cute,* Rachel reminded herself. So instead, she grinned at Taylor and said, "Oh, definitely. In fact, I think you guys are going to make a perfect couple! You'll be so great together."

"So you think he . . . *likes* me?" Taylor asked. "Really?"

"Are you kidding? Of *course* he likes you!" Rachel exclaimed. "Why else would Shane ask you to go to the party tonight? It's not like the dance. I didn't hear about anybody else who's going together."

"It's just hard to believe, you know?" Taylor said. "I'm so used to boys ignoring me. Nobody has ever *liked* me . . . not *like*-liked me, I mean. And all this time Shane has been right there, and then . . . suddenly . . . it happened. Just like that. And he's so sweet, Rach! Do you know what I saw him do the other day? Our English class was doing buddy reading at the elementary school, and he noticed that one of the little kids' shoelaces were untied. Shane sat right down on the floor and tied them!"

"Shane is *such* a nice guy," Rachel said approvingly.

"He really is," said Taylor. "And he *likes* me. Me! This has got to be the craziest thing that has ever happened at Archer Middle School."

"Oh, come on!" Rachel teased her friend. "Shane is *lucky*, T. You're the best!"

"No, you are," Taylor said as she admired her perfect manicure. "My nails look great, Rachel. Thanks."

"*Don't* fidget while I do your hair," Rachel said firmly. "Otherwise, they'll get all smudged."

"I know, I know," Taylor replied. She sat very still as Rachel started pinning back small sections of her hair with sparkly star-shaped clips. "I really, really wish you were going to the party tonight. It's not going to be any fun without you."

"Whatever," Rachel said, rolling her eyes. "You're going with *Shane*. You're going to have the best time!"

"Well, it won't be the same," Taylor replied.

"I'd give *anything* to be there tonight," Rachel said wistfully. "I mean, to *talk* to Brody in person again after all these months . . . and even just to *see* him . . ."

Suddenly, Taylor's eyes brightened. She tried to jump up, but Rachel pushed her back into the chair. "Don't move until your nails are dry!" Rachel scolded.

"Sorry, sorry—but I just had the best idea!" Taylor said. "So maybe you can't go to the party, but that doesn't mean you have to miss it!"

"Huh?"

"I'll have my cell," Taylor continued. "So I can text you the whole time to tell you everything that's happening. And I can send pics! Maybe even a pic of Brody! It will be just like you're there!"

"Really?" Rachel asked. "You don't mind?"

"Of course not," Taylor replied right away. "I was probably going to take a bunch of pictures anyway."

"Then I'd love it!" Rachel exclaimed. "Now I won't

sit alone all night feeling totally left out. Thank you so much."

Taylor waved her blue-nailed hand in the air. "Please. Forget it. It's nothing. All I can say is thank goodness you'll be at the dance on Saturday. Did you talk to your dad about the concert yet?"

Rachel shook her head. "No."

"Rach! The concert is in forty-eight hours. What are you waiting for?"

"Ugh, I don't know," Rachel replied. "I guess if I haven't asked him yet, he hasn't said no yet—and there's still a chance I can go. But if he *does* say no, it's over. And I just don't want to face that. Not yet."

"I get that, but you're running out of time," replied Taylor. Then she glanced at her cell. "And so am I. My mom said I have to eat dinner here before the party, or else she won't let me go. You want to stay? I think we're having something boring like sandwiches since I have to eat fast."

"What, unlimited chocolate fountain isn't good enough for dinner?" Rachel laughed as she reached for her coat. "I have to go, anyway. We're having family dinner tonight. But you look so, so pretty, T. You're going to be the prettiest girl there. Shane is going to lose his mind when he sees you."

"Shut up. You're so nice," Taylor replied, looking pleased. "I will text you the minute I get there. Promise."

"I'll be waiting!" Rachel replied.

The sun was setting in a frosty sky as Rachel walked home. With every step away from Taylor's house, Rachel left a little of her enthusiasm behind. There was a hollow sort of ache in her chest as she wondered if Taylor realized how lucky she was. Sure, Taylor's parents had plenty of rules for her, too, but they weren't nearly as strict as Rachel's dad. And Taylor liked a boy who actually liked her back! For a moment, Rachel wished that her dad was like Taylor's parents. And she wished that Brody was like Shane—just a regular guy at their school, a guy who might actually like her, instead of a superstar who could go out with any girl on the planet.

Then Rachel saw her dad pull into the driveway. He got out of the car, carrying a steaming pizza box. Normally he would only bring home pizza for dinner on somebody's birthday, or if Grandma Nellie was too busy to cook. Pizza was one of Rachel's favorites, and she had to wonder if her dad was making a special effort for their family dinner. Did he remember that tonight was the party at the Chocolate Bar—and remember how much Rachel wanted to go? Was he trying to make it up to her?

. Just like that, Rachel's wishes for a different family and a different crush disappeared. She loved her family. And if Brody were somebody else, he wouldn't be *Brody*.

When she got inside, Rachel's family was gathering around the table. Grandma Nellie was in the middle of serving up a big green salad, and Robbie already had a smear of tomato sauce on his face.

"Just in time, kiddo," Mr. Wilson said heartily. "What do you think about dinner, huh? Surprised?"

"Smells good!" Rachel replied as she sniffed at the air. "Thanks, Dad."

After she sat down, Rachel slipped her cell out of her pocket. Under the table, she set it to vibrate. She wasn't sure when Taylor was going to start texting, but she didn't want to miss a single one.

"So what did everybody do today?" Mr. Wilson asked as he passed around slices of pizza.

"Robbie and I ran so many errands," Grandma Nellie began. "He was such a big boy, helping me at every store!"

Rachel tried to concentrate on the conversation, but her eyes kept drifting toward the clock. *It's five forty-five already. I bet the Chocolate Bar is all set up for the party. I wonder if anyone's shown up yet,* she thought.

Then Rachel heard a car pull up next door. She glanced out the window and saw everything: Mrs. Allen sitting at the wheel, Shane jumping out of the front seat, Taylor following Shane back to the car. Then—Rachel's heart clenched—Shane slid into the back after Taylor. He obviously wanted to sit right next to her.

Rachel's feelings were so jumbled up right then that she could hardly make sense of them. She was thrilled for Taylor—and at the same time, filled with longing for something that she wanted but knew that she would probably never have. The thought of Brody pulling up in front of her house—in, what, a limo?—was so silly that even Rachel couldn't take it seriously.

But that didn't mean she didn't want it to happen. More than anything.

Rachel put down her half-eaten slice of pizza. Suddenly, she wasn't feeling hungry anymore. "May I be excused?" she asked in a quiet voice.

Mr. Wilson looked at Rachel in surprise. "Sure, Rach. Is everything okay?" he asked.

"Sure," Rachel said, but even she could tell that she didn't sound very convincing. "I'm not that hungry, I guess."

"We have chocolate cupcakes for dessert," Grandma Nellie said, trying to tempt her to stay and finish her dinner.

Rachel tried to smile. "Maybe later," she replied.

As Rachel carried her dishes into the kitchen, she felt her phone start to buzz. Could it be a text from Taylor already? Rachel waited to find out until she was back in her bedroom, listening to "Secret Crush" on repeat.

Just got here. Shane looks sooo cute ☺

OMG Rach!! The whole place is closed 2nite just 4 us! There is a velvet rope even!

Rachel smiled at the picture Taylor sent—there was a large sign on the door of the Chocolate Bar that read CLOSED FOR PRIVATE EVENT, and a crimson-colored velvet rope blocking the door.

Our names are on a LIST 2 get in!!

No Brody yet. Maybe he is going 2 make an entrance??

Probably, Rachel thought. *Don't famous people always show up a little late, after everyone else has arrived?*

The next picture that Taylor sent showed the interior of the Chocolate Bar, with its dark purple couches and shimmery gold drapes.

Rach, check out the food! OMG so much chocolate!

Rachel loved the next photo—an elaborate chocolate layer cake covered in gold musical notes. She texted back:

Awesome!! Can u bring me a piece?

Almost immediately, Taylor sent Rachel another picture.

Looooook at charlotte! Soooo pretty!!

Rachel took one glance at the photo of Charlotte in her bright red top and fluttery black skirt and had to agree.

Tell her I think she looks gr8!

Then she waited for another text from Taylor.
And waited.
And waited.
Rachel's fingers clutched her phone as she wondered why Taylor hadn't sent another update.
Then, it came: The text Rachel had been waiting for.

HE'S HEEEEEEEEERRRRREEEEE!

Aaaah! Tell me everything!!!

Trying 2 get a pic. Too many people!!

Rachel tapped her feet in time to Brody's music while she waited for Taylor's next pic—she was too excited to sit still. When it flashed onto the screen, Rachel almost dropped her phone. There he was! The photo was a little blurry, but Rachel would recognize Brody anywhere. His head was tilted to the side so that his face was partially obscured, but Rachel could tell that he was listening intently to the person next to him. The only problem was that there were so many people clustered around Brody that she couldn't quite tell who that was.

Then Rachel noticed a flash of long red hair, and her heart sank.

It was Tammy.

And there was Brody, hanging on her every word. Rachel didn't need to be an expert in body language to analyze the picture: Tammy standing right next to him; Brody leaning toward her; that half smile—part happy, part shy—playing across his face.

It's over, Rachel realized as she stared at the photo. *It was always Tammy.*

And never me.

Trying 2 get a better pic

It got crazy here

Rachel was numb as she texted back.

Don't worry about it. I have homework. Thx T . . . have
fun.

Then she turned off her phone. Not just set it to
vibrate, not just silenced it, but turned it completely off.
Then, with a click of her mouse, she silenced the music.
Brody's music.

What am I going to do now? Rachel wondered. She
really just wanted to curl up in bed and sleep until this
horrible realization stopped hurting so much. Rachel knew
that wasn't possible, though—at least not yet. She still hadn't
finished her homework. But sitting down to study her science
vocabulary was just about the last thing Rachel wanted to do.

Then she spotted the pile of scrapbooking supplies
on her desk.

Without even knowing what she was going to write,
Rachel sat down and picked up a pen. She peeled the
plastic wrapping from the new lined paper Grandma Nellie
had given her and selected a blue sheet. She smoothed it
down on her desk and started writing.

It was only May, but it already felt like
summer. Brody and I were sitting at the bus

stop outside of church, waiting for the bus. And waiting, and waiting, and waiting. Honestly, I didn't want it to ever come. It was so nice to just hang out with him in the sunshine.

Then he said, "It's almost five twenty. I don't think the five o'clock bus is coming. You want to walk?"

We walked west down Linden Street. The sun had started to set, but it was really bright and shining right in my eyes. All I could see were these sparkling spots everywhere, but I tried to walk like normal. Brody was smart; he had sunglasses. Maybe he was already practicing to be a star.

Suddenly Brody grabbed my backpack and yanked me over toward him. I stumbled a little, but he kept me from falling down. And I was thinking, WHAT is going on?

"Sorry," Brody said right away. "There was broken glass all over the sidewalk."

"Oh, thanks," I replied. "I guess I didn't see it. The sun is shining right in my eyes."

"Yeah, it's shining in your hair, too," he said. At least, I think that's what he said. Afterward he

got really quiet, and then he started singing while
we walked. We couldn't really talk while he was
singing, but that was fine with me. It was enough
just to walk beside him and listen to his amazing
voice. I didn't even care about the sun anymore.

Rachel sighed as she put down her pen. And then
suddenly she remembered some lines from "Secret
Crush":

> *Walkin' in the springtime*
> *You shine just like the sun*
> *And when I think about you*
> *Girl, I know that you're the one*

We did that, Rachel slowly realized. *Brody and I
were walking in the springtime. And the sun . . .*

Could it be another clue?

At this point Rachel knew better than to get too
excited. But after focusing on certain lyrics from "Secret
Crush"—the springtime walk, the shining sun, making
music together—the photo of Brody and Tammy suddenly
seemed less convincing.

Rachel turned to her computer and clicked on the music icon. She pulled up *Songs From My Heart* and scrolled through until she reached "Secret Crush." She clicked play and, turning the volume up as loud as she dared, started singing along with "Secret Crush" as she put her scrapbook away. She was ready to tackle her science homework now.

In fact, Rachel was pretty sure she could tackle anything.

chapter 9

BEFORE HOMEROOM STARTED THE NEXT MORNING,
Rachel and Taylor met up with some friends in the main
hall. For the other girls, it was like they'd never left the
Chocolate Bar. They immediately started talking about all
the drama that went down after a paparazzi photographer
sneaked into the Chocolate Bar and started snapping
pictures of Brody. The photographer and Brody's
manager had gotten into a fight, and someone had even
called the police! Rachel was astonished that the paparazzi
had followed Brody to a party with his old friends from
middle school. It made her feel kind of bad for Brody. But
her friends thought it was really exciting. Some of them
even hoped that they'd show up in the pictures that were
posted on a bunch of gossip blogs.

As her friends kept chatting, Rachel slipped away to
go to her locker. It was really awkward to stand there

with nothing to say, and hearing so much about the party made Rachel feel worse about missing it. But as Rachel approached her locker, she realized that someone was waiting for her. Someone with beautiful red hair and a perfect singing voice.

Tammy. Again.

What is she doing here? Rachel wondered, dreading the conversation she was about to have. *Something must've happened at the party. Maybe Brody told her about his feelings . . . and now Tammy wants me to know that she's his crush. That way, I'll be less upset when he tells the whole world.*

"Hey, Tammy," Rachel called out, trying to make her voice sound bright and cheerful. "What's up?"

When Tammy turned around, Rachel noticed right away that she looked a little pale. The sparkle in her eyes seemed dimmer, too.

"Rachel, hi," Tammy said slowly. "How's it going? We missed you at the party last night."

"Yeah, I couldn't make it," Rachel said. "I heard it was fun, though. Did you have a good time with . . . Brody?"

Tammy smiled sadly. "It was amazing to see him

again. He really hasn't changed at all, you know? I mean, his clothes are a little cooler, I guess, but inside he's the same Brody."

It seemed like there was something else that Tammy wanted to say. Rachel waited patiently for her to continue.

"Here's the thing," Tammy finally said. "So . . . I'm not Brody's crush."

Rachel's mouth almost dropped open in shock, but she quickly covered her surprise. "But—but I saw a picture of you guys. Brody looked really happy to see you."

Tammy shrugged. "I think he was really happy to see everyone," she replied.

"I don't know—" Rachel began.

"I do," Tammy interrupted her. "You can just *tell* if somebody's into you, you know? When you like someone, you want to see them. Be near them. Talk to them. And Brody—honestly, Rachel, he was kind of distracted. He kept glancing at the door . . . like he was looking for someone."

"He was probably just looking out for more photographers," Rachel said. As more students arrived for school, she tried to keep her voice down so that no one would overhear their conversation.

"You don't have to do that, Rachel," Tammy said. "I mean, it's sweet and all, but I'm not going to pretend there's still a chance that Brody likes me. Because last night, it was pretty obvious that he doesn't."

"I'm sorry," Rachel said quietly.

Tammy moved her backpack to her other shoulder. "Yeah, well . . . I wish things were different, but . . . it is what it is. But I thought you should know. Anyway, I'd better go. Homeroom starts soon."

"See you, Tammy," said Rachel.

Tammy gave her a little wave, then started to walk away. But after a few feet, she turned around. "Since you were the only girl Brody invited who didn't go to the party . . . maybe he was looking for you," she said.

Then Tammy disappeared into the crowded hallway, leaving a stunned Rachel behind. She stood in the hall for just a moment before she spun around and walked to the principal's office as fast as she could.

"I need to pick up my ticket for Brody's concert," Rachel said breathlessly to the secretary.

After dinner that night Rachel waited for her dad in the living room. It seemed like it took him forever to get

Robbie to sleep, but at last she heard his footsteps walking down the hall.

"Dad," she said right away. "Can I talk to you?"

"Sure, kiddo," her father replied as he sat in his favorite armchair. "What's going on?"

"It's about tomorrow night," Rachel began.

"Right, there's a dance at school, isn't there?" Mr. Wilson said. "Do you and Taylor need a ride?"

"Um, yeah, I mean, I do, but Taylor's going with Shane—"

"Shane? She's going to the dance with a boy?" Mr. Wilson asked in surprise. "I can't believe her parents would let her do that."

A million warning lights started flashing in Rachel's mind, but she pressed on. The concert was in less than twenty-four hours. If she didn't tell her dad about it now, she might not get another chance.

"So the thing is," she continued, "Brody Warner is giving a concert before the dance. Everyone in seventh and eighth grade got a free ticket, and—"

"I don't think so, Rachel," Mr. Wilson interrupted her.

"Dad. Wait," Rachel said, trying to control the frustration in her voice. "You didn't even let me finish—"

"That's because the answer is no," Mr. Wilson replied calmly. "You're too young to go to a rock concert, kiddo. Maybe in three or four years."

"But Dad! It's a huge deal!" Rachel said, raising her voice.

Grandma Nellie entered the living room with a worried look on her face. "Rachel, why don't you tell your dad why it's so important to you?" she suggested gently.

Rachel took a deep breath. She hadn't been planning to tell her dad about this, but if Grandma Nellie thought it was a good idea, maybe she should. The words rushed out of her mouth. "Brody's new album has this song, 'Secret Crush.' And at the concert he's going to tell everyone who she is. It's been big news for weeks. In fact, there wasn't even a dance at school until Brody's concert was announced—"

"Wait a minute," Mr. Wilson said. "You've known about the concert for *weeks* and you're just telling me now? Why didn't you mention it the other day?"

"Carl, hold on," Grandma Nellie spoke up. "Rachel told me about the concert, and I think she should be allowed to go."

Mr. Wilson stared at his mother in disbelief. "Why on

earth would you think that's your decision to make?" he asked.

"Because it was so obvious that you were going to say no without even thinking about it—" Rachel began.

"So you chose to lie to me instead?" Mr. Wilson said. "That just proves my point that you're too young for an event like this."

"You're not letting me finish!" Rachel cried. "I do so much stuff around here and you never notice. It doesn't even matter how much I do because you keep treating me like a five-year-old! I'm *not* too young; I'm really responsible, but *you* just don't pay attention!"

"I don't appreciate that tone of voice," snapped Mr. Wilson. "A responsible person wouldn't keep things from her father or talk to him that way. As punishment, you're not going to that dance tomorrow, Rachel, and you can forget about the concert."

"That's *not fair!*" Rachel yelled. "I'm never allowed to do *anything*! I missed Brody's pool party last summer, I missed Brody's Chocolate Bar party, now I can miss Brody's concert and the Valentine's dance, even though every single one of my friends is allowed to go, and—"

"That's enough, Rachel!"

"It's not enough! Nothing I do is enough!" Rachel cried. "The concert is important to me, Dad! It *really matters* to me. Brody's been gone for *so long* and he's my friend. I miss him! And I've wondered and wondered and now I can finally find out who he likes—I can't believe you're going to make me miss it—"

Mr. Wilson looked confused. Then a sudden understanding dawned on his face. "You don't think *you're* Brody's crush, do you, Rachel?"

All the blood rushed to Rachel's face, burning her cheeks. Stinging tears sprung to her eyes as she realized what her father was really trying to say: *Rachel, there's no way a world-famous superstar could actually like you.*

"No," Rachel said, her voice shaking. "Of course I don't think that. You're right, Dad. Brody Warner wouldn't waste his time on an immature, irresponsible *liar* like me."

"Rachel—"

But it was too late. Rachel was already running down the hall to her bedroom, where it took all her resolve to shut the door quietly instead of slamming it like she wanted to. She curled up on her bed and burst into tears, hiding her face in her pillow. Grandma Nellie knocked two separate times, but Rachel didn't answer. There was nothing that Grandma Nellie could say or do that would make her feel better.

When she was all cried out, Rachel took a deep, trembling breath and wiped her face. She didn't know what to do next. She was afraid to leave her room because she knew her dad must be furious at her. She was too upset to try to explain to him that she hadn't lied about the concert . . . and besides, it was really unfair that he had jumped to the conclusion that she had lied in the first place. The truth was, Rachel was really mad *and* frustrated *and* sad.

She sat down at her computer and decided to check her e-mail.

From: the_real_brody@brodywarner.com

To: friends [list]

Date: February 13

Subject: Tomorrow night

Guys, it was awesome to see you last night. I wish
I had more time to hang out with each one of you.
Let's keep the party going, k? There's a VIP lounge
at the arena and I'll be hanging out there before
the concert. I put your names on the list, so if you
can get to the arena early, stop by and chill. It's on
the second floor—use the far-left stairs. See you
tomorrow!

BRODY

That's great, Rachel thought. *Another chance to see
Brody . . . another chance to find out if Tammy was
right . . . another fun thing my dad will make me miss.*

Rachel deleted the e-mail without bothering to read it
again. Then she turned off the light and went to bed.

chapter 10

IN THE GRAY LIGHT OF DAWN RACHEL'S EYES
snapped open. For a brief, wonderful moment she
remembered that it was Valentine's Day, and in just a
few more hours she would see Brody at the dance. The
identity of Brody's secret crush would be revealed, and all
of Rachel's questions would be answered at last.

Then, like a nightmare, the memory of fighting with
her dad came rushing back. A heavy sadness settled over
Rachel as she realized there would be no concert for
her. No dance. And no time with Brody. What a long,
miserable day stretched out before her. And how would
she get through the evening, knowing what she was
missing? It had been hard enough to sit at home while the
Chocolate Bar party was happening downtown. Tonight
would be about a million times worse.

Rachel walked across her bedroom and listened

carefully at the door. The house was very quiet—so quiet that she was certain that everyone else was still asleep. Moving soundlessly, Rachel crept down the hall to the kitchen to grab a bowl of cold cereal so that she could eat breakfast by herself. Yes, it was Valentine's Day, and that meant that Grandma Nellie would be making heart-shaped pancakes with strawberries and whipped cream—but Rachel didn't think she could choke down a single bite. And she certainly couldn't sit across the table from her father and act like nothing was wrong.

Back in her room Rachel crawled into bed and forced herself to fall asleep again. It was better than the alternative: watching the clock and counting down the hours to the loneliest night of her life.

The next time Rachel awoke, it was to a soft *tap-tap-tap* on her door. She rolled over in bed and waited for the knocking to stop. But when it didn't, she finally got up.

"Grandma Nellie, I just want to be alone right now," Rachel said through the closed door.

"Actually, Rachel, it's me," her dad's voice answered. "Can I come in?"

Rachel hesitated for a moment. She didn't feel ready

to face her dad, not after their terrible argument.

Then he added, "Please?"

Without speaking, Rachel opened the door. Mr. Wilson followed her into the room and sat down at the foot of the bed. Rachel perched on the edge of her desk and waited for him to speak.

"It's a funny thing, being a parent," Mr. Wilson finally began. "It's like having a dozen different pairs of eyes at the same time. Because when I look at you, Rachel, I don't just see you as you are today. I see you when you were nine years old and you had your first solo in the choir, and the way your face glowed with happiness. I see you when you were five years old, on the first day of kindergarten—the way you skipped into the classroom without ever looking back. I see you when you were one, taking your very first steps away from me, and the big grin on your face as you realized, for the first time, what it felt like to be independent . . . for a moment, at least.

"You're growing up so fast, and sometimes it's hard for me to remember that you're not a little girl anymore. Because you're always going to be *my* little girl—no matter how big you are."

Rachel stared at the floor. She wasn't quite sure what to say.

Mr. Wilson sighed. "You have to be patient with your old dad. I'm not very good at this. But I guess what I'm trying to say, Rachel, is that I'm sorry for last night. I'm not proud of the way I handled our argument."

"I'm sorry too," Rachel said. "I wasn't trying to lie to you, Dad. I was always going to tell you about the concert. I just waited too long, I think. Because I guess part of me always knew that you were going to say no, so until I asked, I could at least pretend that there was still a chance."

"But I don't want to be the dad who always says no," Mr. Wilson replied. "I don't want you to feel like you have to keep things from me. And most of all, I'm disappointed in myself for hurting your feelings. About—" Mr. Wilson paused to clear his throat, "about Brody— please understand where my reaction came from. I was honestly so surprised to realize that my sweet little girl is old enough to inspire love songs. But of course you are. And really, what's not to love?"

For the first time all day, Rachel smiled a little.

"I want you to go to the concert and the dance

tonight, Rachel," Mr. Wilson said. "Because I know that you're old enough, and smart enough, to make good decisions—and to take care of yourself. After all, look at how much you do to take care of everyone else around here . . . every day."

Rachel could hardly believe her ears. "Seriously?" she squealed. "Do you mean it, Dad?"

"I do," he replied. "I love you, Rachel. And I hope that you have a wonderful time tonight."

Rachel gave her dad a huge hug and kissed him on the cheek. Then she immediately started texting Taylor. The concert started in less than four hours—and Rachel needed her best friend more than ever!

As soon as she heard that Rachel was allowed to go to the concert, Taylor texted Shane that she would meet him in the VIP lounge. Then she rushed over to Rachel's house and spent the entire afternoon helping her get ready. When Taylor was done, Rachel felt prettier than ever. Her nails were painted the same shade of gold as the sparkly necklace she had borrowed from Taylor, and her crimson top made her cheeks look even rosier than usual. When Mr. Wilson saw Rachel all dressed up for the concert, his eyes got so wide that for a moment, Rachel worried that he was about to change his mind.

But that didn't happen. Instead, her father smiled and said, "You look absolutely beautiful, kiddo."

And now Rachel was standing outside the Archer Arena, staring at hundreds of people who were waiting to get in. Many of them were wearing T-shirts from Brody's last tour.

"This is crazy!" Rachel gasped. "I had no idea there would be so many people here!"

Taylor laughed. "Well, yeah. It's a Brody Warner concert at the biggest arena in northern Minnesota. What did you expect?"

"I don't see anyone we know," Rachel said as she scanned the crowd.

"Shane might already be in the VIP lounge," replied Taylor. "I bet a lot of other people from school will be there too. Come on!"

Rachel's heart started pounding wildly. This was it: the moment when she would finally see Brody again after nine long months. Was she ready? Suddenly Rachel wasn't sure.

Then again—would she ever be?

"Okay," Rachel said. "Let's do this!"

Rachel and Taylor pushed their way through the crowd to the entrance, where a worker scanned their tickets and waved them through.

Taylor peeked at her phone. "Brody's e-mail says to take the far-left staircase to the second floor."

But before they reached the top of the stairs, a large man wearing all black blocked their path. "Can I help you ladies?" he asked. He was polite, but it was clear he meant business.

"Brody, um, invited us—" Rachel started to say.

"We're on the list," Taylor interrupted her. "Taylor Murphy and Rachel Wilson."

The bouncer glanced over his list of names, then nodded curtly and stepped aside. Taylor grabbed Rachel's hand and pulled her into the VIP lounge. It was dimly lit, with large couches and floor-to-ceiling windows that overlooked the arena. Rachel looked around the crowd of her classmates, searching for one person in particular among all the familiar faces. But she didn't see Brody anywhere.

"Do you see him?" Rachel asked Taylor in a low voice. "Is he here?"

"No way," Taylor replied confidently. "Not yet, anyway. Everybody is still acting way too calm. He must not be here yet."

Rachel had to wonder if Taylor was exaggerating. After all, this wasn't some group of random fans. Everyone here had known Brody for years.

"Taylor! Hi!" Shane exclaimed as he hurried up to the girls. "Oh, hey, Rachel. Did you guys just get here?"

Rachel noticed right away that Shane had a single red rose clutched in his fist. *Aaaah!* she thought. *Shane got Taylor a rose! She is going to* freak! *I have to get out of here so that Shane can give it to her in private.*

"Hey, Shane," Rachel said quickly. "I'm going to get a soda. You guys want anything?"

Shane, looking relieved, shook his head. "No thanks."

"Maybe later," Taylor replied, staring at the rose in Shane's hand.

"Okay. See ya," Rachel replied with a little wave as she hurried off to the buffet. She grabbed a cup of soda and a cookie and tried to look casual as she stood by herself. At least nibbling on the cookie gave her something to do.

There was a sudden flurry of excitement near the doors. Rachel craned her neck to see what was going on.

Brody had arrived!

The air in the room instantly felt electrified to Rachel. After all this time, she and Brody were sharing the same oxygen. *He's definitely taller,* Rachel thought. But in every other way, he seemed like the same supercute Brody. One glimpse of his smile was enough to make Rachel feel all fluttery.

Not that he was smiling at *her*, of course. Rachel was pretty sure that Brody hadn't even noticed her standing way off behind the food table. Brody was surrounded by a group of people—his entourage, Rachel figured— that quickly swelled as practically everyone in the room swarmed around them. Rachel squashed the cookie in a napkin and looked around desperately for a trash can. If this was going to be her big reunion with Brody, she didn't want it to happen with a fistful of cookie crumbs.

But even after Rachel had ditched her drink and dessert, she hung back. It felt so weird—so *forced*—to push her way through the crowd, just to be close to Brody. Yet somehow Tammy, she couldn't help but notice, had managed to do just that. She was standing right by Brody's elbow with her head thrown back, laughing at something funny he had said.

So maybe Tammy didn't give up on Brody after all, Rachel thought.

Then Rachel noticed that Brody wasn't really paying attention to Tammy. He was talking to a girl on his other side.

Someone Rachel had never seen before.

Who is *that?* Rachel wondered.

She was almost as tall as Brody, and easily the prettiest girl in the room. With her long shining hair, perfect skin, and beautiful features, Rachel guessed that the girl might even be a model or an actress. She definitely didn't seem to fit in with the rest of the kids.

Then a man came up behind the girl and Brody and tapped their shoulders. He started speaking to them with his head bent low, like he didn't want to be overheard. There was something so intense about the way the three of them stood together that a sudden unsettling pang hit Rachel hard. Her intuition was trying to tell her something—but Rachel didn't want to know what it was.

Rachel couldn't take her eyes off Brody, the girl, and the man. Then, with a jolt of realization, she recognized the man: He was Brody's manager. The one who had sat next to Brody on *The Scoop* and announced the big plan for Brody to reveal his secret crush.

So who was that girl? And what did Brody's manager have to say to her that was so important?

Then Brody's manager cupped his hand around the girl's elbow and led her out of the VIP lounge. But before she left, she glanced over her shoulder and smiled at Brody.

It was a smile that seemed meant just for him.

Rachel could feel her own smile disappearing as she tried to make sense of what she had seen. Shane and Taylor joined her then; now the red rose was in Taylor's hand, and Taylor had never looked happier.

"What are you doing over here?" Taylor demanded. She gave Rachel a gentle push. "Brody's here. Go talk to him! Now's your chance!"

"Did you see that girl?" asked Rachel.

"What girl?" Taylor replied.

Before Rachel could explain, Tammy approached her. "Rachel—can I talk to you?" she asked.

Rachel followed Tammy to the corner.

"Bad news," Tammy said bluntly. "We were both wrong. Did you see her?"

Rachel nodded.

"Well, I overheard Brody's manager. He was telling her where she should sit for the concert and how to react when Brody starts singing to her."

Rachel still didn't say anything.

"You understand what that means, right?" Tammy continued. "It's her. She's Brody's secret crush."

chapter 11

"I KNOW," RACHEL FINALLY REPLIED. WHAT ELSE could she say?

"I'm pretty surprised," Tammy continued. "I really thought his secret crush was going to be someone from our school. It's kind of unfair that they made us all think that! Do you think she's a model? Or maybe she's a singer. I didn't recognize her from anything, so she must not be *that* famous."

Rachel tried to focus on Tammy's words, but all she really wanted was to get out of the VIP lounge for a few moments. She gestured vaguely toward the door, away from Brody and his entourage. "I think I'm going to take a walk."

"Don't go too far," Tammy called after her. "The concert will be starting soon."

Rachel escaped from the VIP lounge and walked a

little way down the hall. She leaned against the wall; the cool, smooth surface felt good against her flushed cheek. It was so much better to be out here to process this news alone, where no one could see her sudden, overwhelming sadness.

You always knew this was possible, Rachel told herself. *Not just possible—probable. And now you don't have to wonder anymore. That will be nice . . . a little break from all the wondering.*

But even as the thought entered her mind, Rachel knew she didn't mean it. She'd rather spend her whole life wondering if it meant that there was still a chance that Brody liked her.

So . . . Rachel thought. *What now?*

She could call her dad. He would pick her up right away, and she could go home and hide out in her room all night, wallowing and feeling sorry for herself. It would be easier than staying here and trying to act like everything was okay. To pretend that she was just fine.

Or she could stay. She could stay for her very first concert and dance, even if she didn't have a date, even if her crush had feelings for someone else. She could dance with her friends and laugh with them and be a part of all the inside jokes and memories that she usually missed out on.

Yes. She would stay.

"Rachel?"

That voice. It was so familiar. But why would—

Rachel turned around.

Brody was standing behind her!

Rachel took everything in: his black T-shirt; his shy half smile; his eyes, shining with a million unasked questions, focused right on her.

"Hey," he said.

"Hey," Rachel replied. She wondered how her voice could sound so normal when her heart was pounding and her hands were trembling.

"You're not leaving, are you?"

"Me? Oh. No. I just came out here for a second," she said. Rachel desperately tried to think of something to say. She had imagined this moment so many times—but now that she had a chance to live it, her mind had gone completely blank.

"So . . ." Brody began. "Do you, um, like the new album?"

"Are you kidding? I *love* it!" Rachel said. "The songs are amazing. I'm so impressed."

"Yeah?" Brody asked. He looked delighted. "Thanks, Rach. That's really nice. What's your favorite song?"

There was no way that Rachel could tell him it was "Secret Crush." Not after seeing Brody's *real* secret crush. "They're all awesome," she said lamely.

There was an awkward silence, as if neither one knew what to say. Brody started drumming his fingers against his leg. Then he cleared his throat. "Well . . . did you figure out who I wrote 'Secret Crush' for?"

"Actually, I did. I saw her when you guys came into the VIP lounge. She's so pretty." Rachel swallowed hard. This conversation was excruciating. Maybe it *would've* been better to leave.

Brody looked at her blankly. "Huh?" he asked.

Rachel nodded toward the lounge. "The girl in the black dress. She looks really into you, too."

Brody was silent for a moment. Then he burst out laughing. "No, no, no. I didn't write 'Secret Crush' about Lucy. I just met her an hour ago."

Now it was Rachel's turn to look confused. "But—"

"She's the backup," Brody explained. "In case my real crush didn't show up tonight. How embarrassing would that be, right? I'm standing on stage singing to an empty chair? So my manager hired Lucy to pretend to be my crush . . . *ugh*, why am I telling you this? It's humiliating."

"No, go on," Rachel said.

Brody took a deep breath. "Greg hired her since my real crush didn't come to any of the other parties I invited her to."

Rachel stared into Brody's eyes. It *sounded* like—but that wasn't possible—there was no way—

Or was there?

"It's you, Rachel," Brody said simply. "It was always you."

Rachel's reaction started as a warm glow in her heart. It spread through every inch of her before finally settling in her smile, as she beamed with happiness. To stand here with Brody—to find out that he actually liked her— was better than a dream come true. It was almost too amazing to believe.

"Seriously?" Rachel asked. "It's me? But—I—I—"

"Are you mad?"

"Mad? How could I be mad? I—"

Rachel wanted to tell Brody that she felt the same way, but the words seemed to get stuck in her throat. She forced herself to say, "I'm not mad. I've actually never been happier."

The relief that flooded Brody's face was instantaneous. He and Rachel stood in the hallway grinning at each other without speaking. There was nothing, in that perfect moment, that needed to be said.

"What was the clue?" Rachel finally asked.

"You didn't figure it out?" Brody sounded surprised. "Did you hear the message at the end of the song?"

Rachel nodded. "But I couldn't understand all the words. It sounded like . . . I don't know . . . 'L-O-L' or something?"

"And that didn't mean anything to you?"

"Well . . . ," Rachel said, confused. "It means laughing out loud, right?"

"And other things," Brody said with a little smile. Then he got serious. "So . . . is it okay? If I sing 'Secret Crush' to you during the concert?"

"Absolutely," Rachel told him.

"So I guess I have just one more question," Brody continued. "Rachel . . . after the concert . . . would you go to the dance with me?"

"Yes. Yes! I would love to!" Rachel exclaimed.

Brody's smile grew bigger and bigger. "Awesome," he said. "I can't believe this is happening. I can't believe you're here. I figured—there's no way she likes me—"

"How could you think that?" asked Rachel.

"It's been such a long time since I saw you last," Brody replied. "Where have you *been*? Why didn't you come to any of the parties?"

"I *wanted* to," Rachel said. "But my dad is pretty strict."

"Maybe I should have e-mailed him," Brody joked. "The whole reason I kept having those parties was because I wanted to see you."

Before Rachel could respond, Brody's manager rushed up to them.

"Brody, there you are," he exclaimed. "I've been looking everywhere. The show starts in ten minutes!"

Then he looked at Rachel and suddenly seemed to understand everything.

"You must be Rachel," the man said. "I'm Greg Pierce. Nice to meet you." He glanced over at Brody. "So . . . is everything a go?"

"Definitely," Brody replied, still grinning.

"Excellent," Greg said. "Brody, you go warm up. I'll take care of Rachel."

Brody looked at Rachel like he didn't want to leave.

CRUSH

"So I'll see you in a little bit," he promised.

"I'll be there," Rachel said as Brody started to leave. "But, Brody—wait—"

He turned around.

"What *does* L-O-L mean?"

Brody smiled mysteriously. "You'll find out soon."

"Rachel, come on," Greg said. "This way."

Greg led Rachel to the front of the arena, where fifteen rows of chairs were set up right in front of the stage. "Your classmates are going to be in these rows," he explained. "And this seat is for you."

Front row. Center. The best seat in the entire arena. And it was reserved for Rachel.

"All the camera guys know that you'll be sitting here, so whatever you do, don't change seats with anyone," Greg continued.

"Camera guys?" repeated Rachel.

"For the Jumbotrons," he replied, pointing at the massive flat-screens hanging from the ceiling. "And the webcast and the TV broadcast, of course. All of Brody's fans around the world will be watching tonight."

Greg turned away to take a call on his headset. "Yeah. Be right there," he said. "Rachel, I've got to run, but enjoy the show—I'm sure I'll see you backstage afterward."

"Thanks," Rachel said as she sat down, hard, in the reserved seat. It was almost too much to take in. Not just the exchange with Brody outside the VIP lounge— *Did that really happen?* Rachel kept asking herself—but everything else, too: the cavernous arena, the crowds of thousands, the front-row seat that was saved just for her. Rachel glanced around the arena with wide eyes. The band was already onstage, warming up. There were sound technicians stationed at a massive control panel and lighting experts climbing ladders to the spotlights overhead. As more and more people entered the arena, it filled with a constant buzzing hum as their voices echoed off the concrete floors. Somehow over the din, Rachel thought she heard someone call her name. She turned around to see Taylor and Shane sitting five rows behind her. Taylor was waving her rose in the air as she tried to get Rachel's attention. Rachel grinned and waved back. Taylor, looking frustrated, frowned and shook her head. Then she held up her phone and pointed at it.

Rachel understood what Taylor was trying to tell her. She checked her cell and realized that in all the commotion, she had missed several texts.

Rach where r u?

Did u leave?

We r going 2 find seats. Will save u 1.

As Rachel was reading them, another text flashed onto the screen.

Come sit w/ us.

Sorry . . . can't

Whaaa? Why not?

Wait a sec . . .

R u the one?!?!?!?!

☺

Suddenly the arena was plunged into complete and total darkness. Rachel's heart started pounding again.

The concert was about to begin!

In a sudden flash of lights, Brody charged onto the stage and launched right into his first song. The audience leaped to their feet, screaming and cheering. Rachel couldn't stop looking at Brody. Performing in front of thousands of people seemed like something he had been born to do, and she had never been more impressed—or felt more proud. *He's amazing,* she thought. *Brody is so much more talented than any of us even knew.* As the concert continued, Rachel found herself swept away by Brody's music until she forgot what was coming . . . almost.

Then Rachel heard the opening chords of "Secret Crush."

A surge of adrenaline made her legs wobbly and her chest tight; Rachel was glad that there was a chair behind her in case she needed to sit down right away. As a hush fell over the audience, Rachel could tell that this was the moment that *everyone* had been waiting for.

"I have a secret
It's hidden in my heart"

Everything else seemed to disappear—the screaming crowd, the flashing lights, the roving cameras, the glowing Jumbotrons. Rachel was only aware of Brody and his music.

*"And it's only getting bigger
Since we have been apart"*

About halfway through the song Brody started walking down the stairs that were on the side of the stage. There was complete silence in the arena as Brody stopped in front of Rachel and their eyes locked. Nothing else mattered. It was just Rachel and Brody, the way it was always meant to be.

Then Brody reached out his hand to Rachel and sang:

*"And when I think about you
Girl, I know that you're the one"*

Brody kept singing as he led Rachel onto the stage. Rachel blinked several times as she tried to adjust to the blinding brightness of the spotlights. When they reached center stage, the music stopped. In the silence, Brody offered something to Rachel: a cluster of green lollipops, tied up like a bouquet of flowers. He leaned close to the microphone and said, clearly, "I'll always save the green L-O-Ls for you."

Rachel recognized the lollipops right away, of course. They were LOL Pops—the same ones from choir practice! And if the writing hadn't rubbed off the wrapper of the green one Brody had given her last year, the very same one that was now in her scrapbook, Rachel might have figured out the clue days ago. As Rachel accepted the bouquet of LOL Pops, Brody grinned and sang:

> "I think about the best times
> Making music together
> And how much I miss you
> Want to hold your hand forever"

Then he tilted his head to the side and raised his eyebrows as he held the microphone out to Rachel! Rachel knew what he was asking her to do. And, strangely enough, she didn't feel a bit nervous, even though she knew that millions of people were watching. After all, hadn't Rachel already sung those very lines about a thousand times?

Rachel paused, took a deep breath, and sang right into the microphone:

> *"Maybe it's crazy*
> *To feel the way I do"*

Brody moved his head close to hers so that they could sing the final words together.

> *"But you're my secret crush*
> *And I hope you like me, too"*

As the last notes faded away, the crowd went wild! Their screams were deafening as glittery confetti rained down from the ceiling, sending sparkling reflections dancing around the arena.

Rachel and Brody stood together in the middle of the stage, waving at the crowd. She glanced at Brody out of the corner of her eye and realized that he was looking at her. Smiling at her—and only her. What she felt then, Rachel knew, would be impossible to put into words, even in her scrapbook. It was like a dazzling explosion of light and color and pure joy; like fireworks for her heart.

As the spotlights began to dim, Rachel and Brody shared a smile that they would remember for the rest of their lives.

The concert may have been over, but for Rachel and Brody, it was only the beginning!

ANGELA DARLING was nicknamed "The Love Guru" by her friends in school because she always gave such awesome advice on crushes. And Angela's own first crush worked out pretty well . . . they have been married for almost ten years now! When Angela isn't busy watching romantic comedies, reading romance novels, or dreaming up new stories, she works as an editor in New York City. She knows deep down that *every* story can't possibly have a happy ending, but the incurable romantic in her can't help but always look for the silver lining in every cloud.

Here's a sneak peek at the next book in the series:

Isabella likes Ryan.

CRUSH

Does he like her too?

Isabella's Spring Break Crush

ISABELLA CLARK POKED AT HER SALAD WITH A plastic fork. Normally she loved talking with her friends at lunchtime, but today it was just making her depressed.

"And our resort has its own private beach," her friend Amanda was saying. She was practically jumping up and down in her seat as she talked. "So we can just walk out of the hotel and right onto the beach. And the temperature there right now is eighty degrees! Isn't that awesome? I am so tired of the cold."

"And the snow," added Jasmine, glancing toward the nearby window. Mounds of winter snow were piled up in the middle school parking lot and along the walkway. Icicles dripped from the bare tree branches. Snowflake flurries swirled around in the freezing wind.

"It's Chicago. It's supposed to be cold in winter," Isabella said, repeating something her dad said often.

It never really made her feel better to hear it, though. She loved the summer when she didn't have to bundle up every day. The summer sun just made everything feel happier.

"Well, I *love* the snow," said Lilly. With her white-blond hair and blue eyes, Isabella always thought she looked like some kind of snow princess from a fairy tale. "I can't believe we're finally going skiing in Colorado! It's going to be awesome."

Jasmine frowned. "We're not going far at all. Mom's taking us to the Buffalo Lodge. It's kind of lame, but at least they have an indoor pool."

Amanda turned to Isabella. "So are you guys doing anything?"

Isabella sighed. "You know we never do. My dad says this year I can help out in his office and make some extra money."

"That's pretty lame too," Lilly remarked, and Amanda shot her a look. "I don't mean that Bella's lame. I mean her dad is lame, you know, for making her work."

"It's okay," Isabella replied glumly. "You're right. It is lame."

"It's not all that bad," Amanda said, trying to cheer

her up. "That way you can buy those great earrings we saw at Sparks."

"Yeah," Isabella said, and then she started poking at her salad again. Amanda was supersweet, and a great best friend. But nothing she said could get Isabella out of her mood.

It just wasn't fair! She was pretty sure that her family was the only one in the whole school who didn't go anywhere during spring break. Things got complicated for the Clarks during this time of year.

For one thing, even though it was "spring break," it still felt like winter in Chicago. Isabella's mom was a pediatrician, and this time of year she was bombarded with kids coming down with the flu.

And it's not like her dad could take them anywhere. Mr. Clark was an accountant, which meant he had to help dozens of people do their taxes before April 15. So he couldn't leave his job either.

"We'll make it up to you in the summer," her mom always said, and it was true—they always went on a nice vacation in the summer. But their last vacation was a distant memory now, and in two weeks all she had to look forward to was filing folders in her dad's office as she watched the snow fall outside.

"Well, the week goes by fast anyway," said Amanda.

Jasmine was scrolling on her phone. "Hey, I forgot that Buffalo Lodge has horseback riding! Maybe it won't be so bad after all."

Lilly leaned in and lowered her voice. "Okay. If you could go on spring break with any boy in our class, who would it be?"

"That's easy. Colin Hancock," Jasmine replied. "He's so cute."

"No way!" Lilly squealed. "I was going to pick him!"

"Well, I think I would want to go with Brian Bender," Amanda said a little shyly.

"Him? He's so nerdy!" Jasmine said.

"That's why I like him," Amanda replied.

Lilly turned to Isabella. "What about you?"

Isabella shrugged. "I don't really know." Which was true. She had never had a real crush on a boy yet. Sure, there were some nice, cute boys in her class, but she would never think of like, *dating* any of them. "Besides, it doesn't matter, because I'm not going on spring break anyway."

Finally the lunch bell rang. Isabella was glad the

conversation was over, but she still couldn't stop thinking about break.

I'll keep working on Mom and Dad, she plotted, as she gathered up her books for her afternoon classes. *There has to be some way to save spring break!*

Have you fallen head over heels for Crush?
Check out these other books in the series!

Lauren's Beach Crush

Maddie's Camp Crush

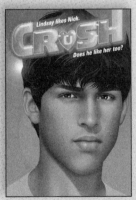
Lindsay's Surprise Crush

Noelle's Christmas Crush

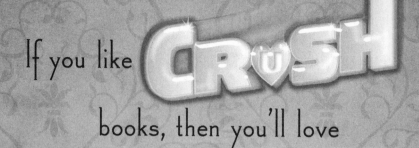